Liquid damage near spine 7/19
TBTCH

CON
ACADEMY

By Joe Schreiber

HOUGHTON MIFFLIN HARCOURT

BOSTON   NEW YORK

To Christina, heart of my heart

Many women do noble things, but you surpass them all.

—Proverbs 31:29

www.hmhco.com

The text of this book is set in Dante MT Std.
Title page illustration © 2015 by Shutterstock.

Library of Congress Cataloging-in-Publication Data
Schreiber, Joe, 1969–
Con Academy / by Joe Schreiber.
p. cm.
Summary: Con man Will Shea may have met his match in scammer Andrea
Dufresne as they make a high-stakes deal that will determine who gets to stay
at Connaughton Academy, one of the most elite and privileged preparatory
schools in the country, and who must leave.
ISBN 978-0-544-32020-8
[1. Swindlers and swindling—Fiction. 2. Conduct of life—Fiction.
3. Preparatory schools—Fiction. 4. Schools—Fiction.] I. Title.
PZ7.S37913Con 2015
[Fic]—dc23
2014014198

Manufactured in the U.S.A.
DOC 10 9 8 7 6 5 4 3 2 1
4500539919

"Yours, sir, if I mistake not, must be a beautiful soul—one full of all love and truth; for where beauty is, there must those be."
—Herman Melville, *The Confidence-Man* (1857)

"Excuse me, is that man actually royalty?"
—*Dirty Rotten Scoundrels* (1988)

ONE

THIS IS HOW I ALWAYS START:

"My name is Will Shea. You can probably tell that I'm not from around here."

It's 11:07 a.m. and I'm looking out on a classroom of eighteen faces, their expressions ranging from curious to indifferent to the flat-out glassy-eyed stare that you see only in closed-head-injury victims. Somewhere off to my right, Mr. Bodkins, my English Lit teacher, leans back in his swivel chair with his arms crossed. He's dressed in a charcoal suit and skinny tie, his hip-in-the-'90s haystack-style haircut going gray around the temples, and I'm guessing he probably has a trunk full of unpublished novels stretching back into his undergraduate years. Steam from his Connaughton Academy coffee cup floats above his head like an empty thought bubble.

From the back, somebody coughs, and I realize the silence has gone on too long. Glancing over my shoulder at the wall behind me, I can feel the heat rising in my face, flushing into my cheeks and making the tips of my ears turn red.

"I was born in a part of the world most of you probably have never heard of," I say, "a tiny island called Ebeye. It's out in the middle of the Pacific, about two thousand miles southwest of Hawaii."

"Island living," somebody from the back mutters. "Sounds pretty sweet," and there's a vague murmur of disinterested laughter that Mr. Bodkins chooses to ignore.

"It's a very small country," I say. "My parents were missionaries there, but . . ."

Somebody giggles, and I falter, letting the rest of the sentence hang there, and glance over at Mr. Bodkins, but he just nods.

"It's all right, Mr. Shea. Take your time."

I draw in a breath, feeling the knot of tension tightening in the room, a kind of silent impatience that you find only in the uppermost echelons of American wealth. These are the children of the elite. Row upon row of entitled faces framed by generations of flawless breeding, exquisite genetics, perfect teeth—future masters of the universe gathered here to prepare for their college years and a lifetime of the best of everything.

Connaughton Academy is consistently ranked among the top five private schools in the nation, which easily puts it in the top ten worldwide. They all wear designer uniforms at Connaughton—tailored suits for the boys, skirts for the girls —but mine wasn't ready when I got here, so I'm still wearing the jeans and off-brand hoodie that I arrived in this morning. Somewhere outside the arched floor-to-ceiling windows, the great oaks and maples of Connaughton's campus blaze with the oranges, reds, and yellows of New England fall.

"I'm here on a scholarship." The words come out of me in an angular lump, like I've coughed up a wooden alphabet block. "After my parents died, the people from our church put together a fund to send me here . . ."

In the back row, somebody starts to snore, absurdly loud. I can see the snorer from here, a lanky blond kid with perfect skin and Abercrombie bone structure, sprawled out behind his desk with both legs stuck straight out in the aisle and his head flung back. Everybody around him erupts into laughter, and the kid sits up, shrugging one shoulder and blinking innocent blue eyes. I glance back at Mr. Bodkins, who tries to speak over the roars and hoots.

"That's enough, Mr. Rush," he says, but his voice is so tentative that I can barely hear it. He nods at me. "Go ahead, Mr. Shea. Please finish."

I draw in another breath. If I have to stand up here much longer, my face is going to burst into flames.

That's when I notice the girl.

She's sitting three rows back with her hands under her desk, and I realize that she's texting without looking down at the screen. She's pretty in a way that I haven't seen before, like a Jazz Age flapper in the post-*Twilight* era, jet-black hair swept away from her forehead in a smooth, precise wave, and very dark, full eyes. Skin as pale as milk. Up until this moment she's been paying zero attention to me, but now I see her slipping the iPhone into the pocket of her skirt so that she can give me one hundred percent of her focus. Her lips are very red, almost shiny, and there's something in her unblinking stare I can't read.

"Continue, Mr. Shea," Mr. Bodkins drones from behind his coffee cup, and now even he sounds like he's drifting off. "You're doing fine."

I swallow hard. "I know that I'm lucky just to be here at Connaughton," I say. "I mean . . . I just hope . . ." I shake my head. On the opposite wall, the hands of the antique clock seem to have frozen in place. "That's it."

Mr. Bodkins nods one more time, a mercy killing if ever there was one.

I make my way back to my seat through stony silence.

In the dining hall that evening, she walks right over to me — the dark-haired girl from class.

"It's Will, right?" She sits down close enough that I can smell her perfume, something faint and musky, with a hint of creaminess, like vanilla. It mixes well with her body chemistry, the natural scent of her skin, as she offers her hand. "I'm Andrea Dufresne."

"Oh," I say, and look up, smiling, and we shake. Her grip is cool, smooth, and firm, with scarlet fingernails. "Nice to meet you."

"Likewise," she says, and for a second we just sit there across from each other, neither of us saying anything while the rest of the students chatter around us, largely ignoring their food. According to the material that the admissions office sends out, Connaughton offers a half-dozen dining options every meal, with vegan and dietary-specific choices. There's a farmers' market on Saturdays, featuring locally grown produce, along with luaus in the spring and fall, and gourmet representations of all different nationalities throughout the year, "spotlighting our culture of diversity," although the only diversifying that's going on here is in stock portfolios. It's the only boarding school in the country that routinely poaches its chefs from Michelin-starred restaurants in New York, Paris, and Hong Kong. Picking up my fork, I look down at the thin-cut prime rib arranged on my plate along with fresh asparagus and new potatoes, spear a piece of everything together, and pop it into my mouth. It tastes so good that for a second my tongue doesn't know what to do with it, like a foreign language composed exclusively of deliciousness.

"Not a talker," Andrea says after a moment. "That's cool." She's got some kind of complicated salad in front of her, something involving grilled salmon and slivered avocado, but for the moment she doesn't seem particularly interested in it. "So what do you think of Connaughton so far?"

"This place?" I chew, swallow, and shake my head. "It's unreal. It's a dream come true."

"You like it?"

"Are you kidding me?" I motion toward the kids around us, one sweeping gesture that I hope takes in the campus, the dorms, the student library that supposedly contains an original Gutenberg Bible—everything from the riding stables to the duck pond to the oh-so-secluded wedge of New Hampshire coastline where the sailing club keeps its boathouses—all the sights that my tour guide showed me this morning. "I'm still in a state of shock."

She sits back and trims off a bit of salmon. "Not much like home, huh?"

"Um, no."

"What's the name of the island that you came from, again? eBay?"

"Ebeye," I say, and then I realize she's joking and manage a smile of my own. "It's part of the Kwajalein Atoll in the Marshall Islands."

"And you were born there?"

"Yep."

"No offense, Will" — she cocks her head slightly to one side — "but you don't look like a native islander."

"My parents moved back there when my mom was pregnant with me." After picking up my fork, I shift my food around on my plate, forming complex algebraic equations with my asparagus and potatoes. It gives me something to look at besides Andrea's penetrating stare. "My grandmother was Polynesian, and my mother was born there — she met my dad in medical school, and they went back to work at the public health clinic." My fork tumbles from my fingers and hits the plate with a clank. "You don't want to hear this stuff."

"You're right," she says. "Shut up, already."

I smile again and it's actually easier this time, closer to natural. She gazes at me straight-faced and takes a bite of egg, chewing slowly, thoughtfully.

"So, what?" she says. "You're going to make me squeeze it out of you?"

"You're serious? You actually want to hear my whole life story?"

A sigh, accompanied by the slightest of exasperated eye rolls. "Okay, Coy Boy, in case you haven't noticed, you're swimming in a sea of boring rich kids whose backgrounds are so identical that if they intermarry, their offspring might be born with eleven fingers," she says. "So yeah. Color me captivated."

"Okay," I say. "Back in the fifties—have you ever heard of the Bikini Atoll?"

"Sounds vaguely familiar."

"It's an island chain in the middle of the northern Pacific Ocean. The government dropped a fifteen-megaton dry-fuel thermonuclear hydrogen bomb on the island back in 1954."

Her eyes get big. "Seriously?"

"It was the most powerful nuclear device ever deployed," I say, "about a thousand times more powerful than the ones *Enola Gay* dropped on Hiroshima and Nagasaki to end World War Two. Radioactive fallout from the mushroom cloud poisoned the entire Marshall Islands chain for more than seven thousand square miles of the Pacific. Eventually Greenpeace got involved, and islanders from all the surrounding areas started evacuating to Ebeye, but it was too late for most of them. They were already dying of radiation poisoning . . . including my grandmother."

"Whoa," she says, and most of the smart-aleck bravado has gone out of her voice. "That really happened?"

I nod, staring down at my meal. "My mom left the island to come to the States when she was a teenager, but she promised her mother she'd get medical training and go back—to help where she could. By the time she finished med school, her mom had passed away." I glance up, just for a second. "I never knew her."

"What about your parents?" Andrea asks. "Were they . . . ?"

I look back down at my plate. "There was an accident. A small plane—they were flying antibiotics to a children's orphanage on a nearby island, but the weather conditions weren't ideal. They knew the risks—"

My voice breaks off and I push my chair back and stand up.

"I'm sorry," I say, and my voice sounds thick and awkward. "This is stupid. You don't even know me and here I am—"

"Will." Andrea reaches out and takes my hand, holding on. Her fingers feel different from when we shook hands—warmer somehow, and soft. "Just chill, okay?"

"It's just . . ." I sink back down into my seat. "Everybody here has been so nice. And I've never been anywhere like this before." I take in a breath. "It feels unreal. Like a dream."

Andrea just watches me with that same quiet, inscrutable interest. "When you were in class today, you kept looking over your shoulder. Why?"

"I was looking for a map," I say. "I just . . . I thought maybe I could at least show everybody where I came from. I mean"—I shake my head—"I know it was English Lit and not Geography, but I thought it would be cool if I could at least point out how far away Ebeye is from . . . all of this."

Andrea is still holding on to my hand, and her voice is soft now too.

"I've got a map in my room," she says.

My dorm is closer, so we end up walking over there instead. As a late transfer student, I've got my own little single at the end of the first floor of Cardiff Hall, one of the oldest dorms on campus. According to the housing brochure, it was built in the early 1900s in the Arts and Crafts style, all oak and dyed leather, with Prairie School bronze sconces on the walls and Gustav Stickley chairs in the lobby. Old money, and lots of it.

"They put you on the first floor?" Andrea asks.

"I don't like heights."

We follow the hallway to my room, which I unlock with the heavy brass key that the housing officer gave me earlier today with an air of weighty solemnity.

"I haven't really had a chance to unpack," I say apologetically as we step inside. The room still feels vacant, with just a few framed photos on the otherwise empty desk. Andrea stands there looking at them, picking up a faded beach photograph of a happy couple standing next to a palm tree with a two-year-old boy between them.

"Your folks?" she asks.

"Uh-huh."

"Your mom's so young." She holds on to the photo for a long moment before putting it back. "They look happy."

"We were."

"You must miss them."

I turn and look out the window. It's dark out now, and I can hear the wind off the ocean, rustling through the leaves. A lonely, restless sound.

"I was going to show you this," I say, opening my backpack and unzipping an inside pocket to pull out a battered old map so I can point to the tiny flyspeck of land in the middle of the Pacific. "Here—this is me."

Andrea comes up behind where I'm standing and reaches around past me to the map, and all of a sudden I'm acutely aware of the closeness of her body heat as her red fingertip traces its way across all that endless blue.

"Here?" she says.

I nod.

"It's so tiny."

"Just a speck on the map."

"Like it's hardly there at all," she says.

There's nothing to say to that, so I just stand with my head cocked slightly toward the window, waiting to see what's going to happen next.

"Will?"

I turn to glance at her. "Yeah?"

"Here's the thing."

"Uh-huh?"

"Your whole life story . . . ?"

"Yes?"

"I don't buy a word of it."

For a moment, my world goes pin-drop silent. Somewhere, a clock ticks. I stare at her, blinking. "What?"

"I don't think you've ever seen *South Pacific*, let alone actually lived there." She's smiling widely now, grabbing hold of my hand as she glances back at the framed photo on my desk. "And if this picture was taken anywhere besides Florida, I'll tear it out of the frame and eat it."

"Wait," I say, frowning. "I don't understand."

"Oh," she says, "I'm pretty sure you do."

"But—"

"I admit," she says, "you had me going at first. It takes a lot of guts to stand at the front of the class wearing those clothes . . . and the whole atomic-testing thing was a nice touch. You've got the routine down, I'll give you that."

"Hold on," I say. "You actually think . . . I'm making all this up?" Now I'm drawing my hand away from hers, stepping back fast enough that the map falls to the floor between us, where it lands half underneath the radiator. "You think I somehow convinced the admissions board to let me into this school?"

"Not just the admissions board," she says, and she's still smiling. "I think you've got *everybody* fooled." She pauses, and her eyes shimmer just a little, deep inside the pupils. "Well. Almost everyone."

"The people from my village . . ." I say, lowering my gaze. "They warned me that when I came here, there would be those who wouldn't understand."

"Oh, please," she says, "give it a rest, okay?"

And she just stands there in front of me, arms crossed, not saying anything, just waiting, until I finally let out a deep breath. It feels like I've been holding it inside for a very long time, and once I'm completely deflated, I realize that I've sat down on the floor of the room.

"Florida?" I say. "Seriously, you *recognized* that as Florida?"

"Fort Lauderdale, I'm guessing," Andrea says. "And that's just the beginning."

TWO

So I get out my refurbished MacBook and tell her the truth.

It takes twenty minutes for me to show her how I hacked into the admissions board's system to fabricate my transcripts and transfer records. Another ten minutes to unzip the hidden lining of my backpack and pull out forged letters of recommendation and income tax forms with the fake notarization stamps and official seals that I hand-stained with Earl Grey tea bags to get the exact right shade of brown. Throughout it all she sits on the edge of my bed, holding the documents up to the light, inspecting the markings and signatures.

"This . . . is . . . unbelievable," she says, and looks at me with what I'd like to think is newfound fascination, although it's probably just a species of shock that medical science hasn't classified yet. "I mean, was *any* of what you told me true?"

"Well . . ." I have to stop and think about it. "My first name really is William," I say, pointing at one of the forms. "See?"

"Anything else?"

"I was telling the truth about never having been anywhere like this before," I say. "We're a long way from the South Ward of Trenton, New Jersey, that's for sure. But everything else I told you" — I nod at the paperwork and the laptop — "was pretty much, you know . . ."

"A big fat lie," she says, like she still can't wrap her head around it.

I shrug. "I was going to say easy, but yeah."

"You've done this before?"

"This is the third school I've gone to." The first two — Horace Mann and Exeter — ended badly, when some inconsistencies in my record were discovered by a sharp-eyed admissions officer, and I've since stepped up my game.

"*Why?*" Andrea asks.

"Why?" Now *I'm* confused. "As in, why would anyone want to attend a private academy with its own airstrip and private jet?"

"It's a helipad," she says. "And that's not the point."

"Okay, maybe you haven't taken a look around you lately? This place is Valhalla. It's the hall of the gods."

"I know what Valhalla is, thanks."

"My point is, even if you guys didn't have a model stock-trading floor so students could learn about the commodity market, it's totally obvious that this is where winners are born and bred. All I did was reinvent myself to fit in. It's the American way."

"Lying about who you are?"

"Semantics," I tell her. "You mean to tell me your great-great-grandparents didn't change their names at Ellis Island?" I hold up my hands. "Oh, wait, your great-great-grandparents probably *owned* Ellis Island . . ."

"My ancestors . . ." she starts, and her voice trails away. "Again, that's not the point. What you did is different."

"How?"

Andrea changes her approach. "What about *your* parents? Your *real* parents, I mean. What do they think about all of this?"

"Let's just say . . ." I glance at the framed photo of the three of us on the desk. "When it comes to family, sometimes the myth is better."

And to my surprise, she nods as if that makes some kind of sense to her. "I'm assuming you've got some kind of long-range plan, at least?"

"Absolutely," I say. "As rich and ambitious as your fellow classmates are, some part of them is dying to help a poor, disenfranchised missionary kid from the Pacific Islands find his way in the big, scary world. Which is why, by winter break, one of them is going to invite me to spend the holidays with his family in Davos, or St. Barts, to show off to Mummy and Daddy how he's learning to help those less fortunate than him. And by next summer, I'll practically have been adopted into the family. I'll do a summer internship at somebody's law office, maybe a clerkship on Capitol Hill. A year from now I'll be applying to Harvard with everybody else. After that, law school or business school, and a job at one of the white shoe firms in Manhattan. Hello, Fortune Five Hundred."

"Impressive," she says. "You've really got us all figured out, don't you?"

I shrug. "If there's one thing more reliable than greed, it's pity."

"What is that, your family motto or something?"

"Hey, I'm a realist."

"And how old are you, again? Forty?"

"Look," I say, "if I can help tomorrow's captains of industry sleep soundly at night with their white liberal guilt, then I call it a win."

"Meanwhile, you've got no sense of guilt whatsoever . . . ?"

"Why should I? I'm not hurting anybody."

She's just looking at me, and I can't read her expression anymore.

"Okay." I let out a sigh. "If you're going to rat me out, I'd appreciate a little advance notice so I can pack my stuff. I mean, this is a great school and everything, but it's not worth getting sent to juvenile detention over."

"Will?"

"Yeah."

"Relax," she says, and puts her hands on my shoulders. "You're just about the most interesting thing that's happened to this place in sixty years. I'm not going to rat you out."

I feel the way she's holding on to my shoulders and realize she's right. Things around here just got a lot more interesting. "So I hear there's a Homecoming dance coming up in a couple of weeks?"

Andrea doesn't say anything at first, just slips me a smile in return as she turns and starts toward the door.

"One step at a time," she says. "Meanwhile"—she pauses to take one last look at the framed photo of the happy family on my desk—"your secret's safe with me."

THREE

I'M TOTALLY ASLEEP, BURIED UNDER THREE LAYERS OF BLAN-
kets, when a fist pounding on the door shoots me fifty stories straight up into stark reality. It's late, or really early
—I can't tell. The glowing blue numerals next to my head read
1:11.

"Wake up, Mr. Humbert," a harsh voice orders from out in
the hall. "Open the door. Right now."

I sit up, kicking off the blankets, and swing my legs around,
still half asleep and dreaming of room service at the Ritz-
Carlton. The bare wooden floorboards are ice-cold beneath
my feet. By the time I'm standing up, shoving my toes into my
slippers, whoever's knocking has already got a key rattling the
lock, and the lights suddenly blaze on, making me squint at
the blue-uniformed figure barging toward me.

Things go from bad to horrible without so much as a detour
in the direction of worse. The tall bald guy in front looks like
a cop, but then I realize he's campus security, followed by a
distinguished man with a trimmed beard and a rich burgundy
bathrobe with the Connaughton insignia emblazoned on the
breast. Something about his pinched, sophisticated face makes
him look more infuriated than the security guard, if that's
even possible.

"Get up, Mr. Humbert," the distinguished man snaps. "Pack your things. You're leaving Connaughton. Tonight."

"Hold on," I say. "What's going on?" Maybe if I blink my eyes fast enough, I can blame this whole thing on a misdiagnosed seizure disorder. "Who's Mr. Humbert, and who are you?"

"I'm Dr. Melville," he says. "I'm the head of the school here, which I thought you might have realized by now. And *this* is what's going on."

He thrusts in my face a folder with a profile sheet clipped to the top, and I see just enough of it to recognize my own photograph staring back at me. The picture is two years old, the most recent one that the New Jersey Department of Human Services has access to—not my best angle. The backwards Yankees cap and surly you're-not-the-boss-of-me smirk don't help. "I assume this looks familiar?" Dr. Melville sneers.

"Where did you get this?"

"I got an angry call from a headmaster down in New York, at the institution that you listed as your last school. Your transcript papers came back. Nobody has ever heard of Will Shea. But the State of New Jersey knows all about Billy Humbert." Dr. Melville points beyond the window. "There's a car waiting for you outside."

"Get packing," the security guard orders. It's his one line in this poor excuse for a crisis, and he delivers it with disgruntled gusto.

"Okay. Just"—I glance around the room—"give me a second to get dressed, okay?"

"You've got two minutes."

I nod and shut the door after them, turning back to the window.

This is why I always get a room on the first floor.

Ninety seconds later, I'm sprinting across campus in my bedroom slippers, making for the main gate at a dead run with all my earthly belongings in a backpack flapping against my shoulders. At least there's a full moon to keep me from crashing into the trees.

I don't recommend running cross-country in slippers, especially not in the freezing cold of late October, when your toes go numb first. Twice I trip over tree roots and once almost collide with a giant statue of the founder of the school, Lancelot Connaughton himself, one hand extended boldly toward the future. By the time I get across the lacrosse field, reach the gate, and toss my backpack over, I've got so many twigs and branches stuck to my legs that I'm wearing my own forest camouflage, which actually proves handy when the sidelight of the campus security SUV waiting outside the gate swings around and hits the ground just in front of me.

I lie there on my stomach with my heart pounding in my chest. My lungs feel as if a pair of cackling pyromaniac twins are setting off Roman candles inside them. Time has now officially stopped. Then, approximately one eternity later, the headlights finally drift away, and I pick myself up and brush myself off, slipping into the woods alongside the road that runs toward town.

After I'm sure the coast is clear, I stumble out of the trees and onto the pavement, where the walking is easier, or at least doable. It's a six-mile trek to town, but I can make it on adrenaline alone. I can probably scrape together the cash for the next bus back to Trenton, and by the time I arrive, I should have some kind of plan.

I hope.

I've been walking for a half hour when a sports car comes flying around a curve, barreling straight at me, tires screeching to a halt less than a foot away from my shins. It's a foreign job, some kind of low-slung coupe with one headlight out, and the driver who stumbles out of it looks like he's got only one functional headlight himself. For a second he just stands there in the middle of the road with his tie yanked down and his shirttails hanging below his sweater vest, blinking at me with the bleary, slack-jawed disbelief of a man whose ventricles are currently pumping more Glenfiddich than blood.

"Who . . . ?" he manages, in a whiskey-fueled slur, and I realize who it is. *"Shea?"*

"Mr. Bodkins?"

"What . . ." My now former English teacher leans a little against the side of the car, peering at me through narrow eyes. "What are you doing out here in the middle of the night?"

"I was . . ." I realize that he doesn't know anything about what happened and I'm free to extrapolate at will, as it were. Not that it matters now. "I was headed into town."

"Now?"

"I need to get to the bus station. There's been an accident back on the island, and I need to get home as soon as I can."

"Is everything all right?"

"I'm not sure," I say. "The headmaster woke me up in the middle of the night." In the midst of another massive lie, a little truth trickles through my system like a cool sip of water. "I had to leave right away." More truth—this stuff could get addictive. "There wasn't a moment to lose."

"So you're *walking?*" Mr. Bodkins slides a little down the hood of the car, catches himself, and stands upright again. "You need a lift?"

I hesitate, wondering if I should entrust my life to a man who looks like he's spent the last four hours marinating himself in single-malt scotch in one of the town's three taverns, and decide I don't have much choice. It's cold and my legs already feel like overcooked rotini.

I climb in.

Five minutes later we're careening through the countryside, flying past maples and stone fences at eighty-five miles an hour like Robert Frost on speed. The inside of Mr. Bodkins's car reeks of cigarettes and scotch, and there are great swollen drifts of uncorrected English themes piled on the back seat, where they spill and tilt with every twist and turn. Driving this fast seems to have sobered Mr. Bodkins up considerably, and he handles the vehicle with what used to be called aplomb, a Camel Light clamped between his teeth and both hands locked on the wheel. Somewhere inside the glowing dashboard, in stark defiance of all this automotive chaos, Miles Davis is finding his way, softly and mournfully, through "'Round Midnight."

"Too bad you have to leave so soon," Mr. Bodkins says, the cigarette twitching between his teeth, and he turns to glance at me. "You *are* coming back, aren't you, Mr. Shea?"

"I don't know." Right now I'm just hoping to survive the trip to town. I'm gripping my seat belt with my backpack tucked between my knees and praying that the road stays straight in front of us, or at least unobstructed by wildlife. If Bambi wanders out in front of the car while we're driving at this velocity, there won't be much left of him but a venison-flavored grease spot.

"We don't get many scholarship students," Mr. Bodkins says. "Besides Andrea, you might be our only one."

I sit up and look over at him. "What did you just say?"

"Andrea Dufresne—you remember her from English Lit." His hand fumbles in the dark for a bottle, and then, realizing that I'm watching, he takes the stick shift instead and changes gears. "Dark-haired girl? Kind of pasty? Looks like she sleeps in a coffin?"

"What about her?"

"She came here on a scholarship too, just like you."

I'm still looking at him. Suddenly I have forgotten all about my seat belt and my backpack and the road in front of us. "Really."

"Oh yeah. Kind of a similar story to yours, actually. She's an orphan, technically a ward of the state. Her parents were

U.S. foreign aid workers in some poor country in the Balkans, killed by friendly fire, I think . . ." Mr. Bodkins shakes his head, as if there are a couple loose facts rattling around inside his skull like Legos and he is trying to get them to attach together. "I can't remember the name of the country now. She wrote a whole paper about it last year. Gave her a B-plus on it. Solid work."

"And how long has she been here?"

"Came in as a sophomore. Made a lot of friends already, though."

"I bet she has," I say.

Mr. Bodkins must have noticed the slight change in my tone, because he turns to look at me. "Are you all right, Will?"

"Can we turn around?" I say. "Back to Connaughton?"

"I thought you had to fly home as soon as possible."

"I do." I just nod, staring out the windshield into the night. "But there's something back there that I need to take care of first."

FOUR

WHEN ANDREA STEPS OUT OF THE BATHROOM AT seven a.m. in a pink fluffy bathrobe and flip-flops with her bucket of toiletries in hand, I'm standing there, leaning against the opposite wall. For a guy who has been up all night and is still wearing the same clothes, I'm feeling surprisingly composed. Spiffy, even.

"How was your shower?" I ask. "I hear the water pressure here is amazing."

"*Will?*" To her credit, she doesn't show more than a flicker of surprise. It's there, and just like that, it's gone, a magic trick of perfect self-control. She even manages a crooked little smile. "What are you doing here?"

"What, you mean as opposed to being driven away in the back seat of a campus security vehicle?" I shake my head. "Sorry to disappoint you."

"I don't know what you're talking about."

"Bravo," I say, giving her a polite little golf clap, keeping it as quiet as possible. It's early, and most of her fellow residents haven't emerged from their rooms yet. We've got the hallway to ourselves, which was how I'd hoped it would be. "And here I thought *I* was a pro."

She makes a little show of glancing up and down the

hall. "You know," she says, lowering her voice to the range of hushed confidentiality, "you really shouldn't be here. This is an all-female dorm. It's locked for a reason."

"Yeah, well. I found an open window in the laundry room."

"You could get in trouble just for being here."

"So now all of a sudden you're a stickler for rules?" I take a step toward her, just to see if she'll retreat, but she stands her ground. "That's really fascinating, considering you've been breaking them yourself for the past year."

Andrea just looks at me. She's not smiling anymore. In fact, I think I see a slight crease of a frown on her forehead. "Will, are you okay? Maybe you hit your head crawling through that window or something."

"You know," I say, "it's no wonder you were able to pick up on my game so quickly. You've been running one of your own for the past year. That's why you couldn't wait to get me out of here, so I wouldn't horn in on your action." I shake my head, and the smile on my face is one of genuine admiration. "What a colossal idiot I was, thinking that I could somehow con *you*."

Andrea cocks her head just slightly. The shadowed pucker of a frown has become a truly agitated scowl. "I think you better leave right now, before you find yourself in an even worse situation than you already are."

"A poor scholarship student from a displaced village in the Balkans?" I say. "Really? Who forged *your* transcripts and tax records, Andrea Dufresne? And how did you really get into Connaughton?"

"That's it," she says, and turns to walk away. "I'm calling security."

"Good," I say. "That way they can drive us *both* to the bus station. You'll be on your way back to Tuscaloosa by lunchtime."

That stops her cold, just like I'd hoped it would. When she finally turns around, all the remaining confidence in her face has drained away, and she stares at me for a long moment. I realize that I'm seeing her without makeup, and she's actually much prettier this way—even though she looks like she's going to haul off and take a swing at my head with her shampoo bucket.

"So what do you want?" she whispers, and even her voice sounds different now, tinged with a Southern drawl. "A medal?"

"No," I say. "Just five minutes of your time."

Her gaze flicks right and left again, so quickly that I can barely track the movement of her eyes, and she grabs my wrist. "Come on," she growls under her breath. "Before somebody sees us here."

Her room is immaculate, walls decorated with Klimt prints and framed antique maps and black-and-white Ansel Adams shots of the Grand Canyon. Hardcover leather-bound books with silver and gold titles embossed on the spines sit on bookshelves. It's totally Crate & Barrel by way of Restoration Hardware. There's a cello case in the corner, next to a metal stand with sheet music spread out on it, all of it very deliberately arranged and, to my newly enlightened sensibilities, totally fake. But at least the room smells like girl, like hair product and moisturizer and Yankee Candle, and when I sit down on the already-made bed, she gives me a grimace of distaste.

"Don't bother making yourself comfortable," she says. "You're not staying."

"Oh, you're not going to kick me out," I say.

"What makes you so sure?"

"Because I've got your number and you know it." I unzip my bag and pull out my laptop, powering it up. "First of all, admit to yourself that what you're running here is a dead-end game."

Andrea blinks at me, then nonchalantly turns to the mirror to begin brushing her still-damp hair, combing it out in long black waves. "How do you figure that?"

"Think about it," I say. "What's your real payoff here? You're going to graduate this year, and then what? Your GPA isn't exactly Ivy League."

"Excuse me?" She stops brushing her hair and turns to stare at me. "How do you know about my GPA?"

"Let's not kid each other," I say, and turn the computer so that she can see the page I'm on. "I told you I've already hacked into the school's mainframe. Security around here is strictly Chuck E. Cheese. I practically sneezed my way through their firewall."

"Let me see that," she says, but I pull the MacBook away from her, beyond her reach. "You can't just snoop through people's transcripts."

"You're right," I say. "It's *dishonest*. I feel so dirty." I look around the room. "Got any coffee?"

She glares at me, simmering in silence. "There's Red Bull in the fridge," she says finally. "You can get it yourself."

"Look." I walk over to the little dorm refrigerator in the closet, pull out a can of Red Bull, and crack it open. "All I'm saying is, there's no payoff. What happens after you graduate? You're back at square one again, right?" I glance at the cello case in the corner. "Or were you planning on conning your way into Juilliard, too? I hear they're a little more difficult to snooker."

"Who says I have to con my way in?"

"So you're really that good?" I stand up and start walking over to the instrument. "You want to play me something? Adagio for Scam Artists in B Major?"

"It doesn't matter," Andrea says, "because as soon as I tell Dr. Melville that you're still here—"

"I'll tell him what I know about you," I say, "and we'll both end up doing our senior year in public school. So it looks like we're stuck with each other."

"No."

"Excuse me?"

"I said no." She settles into her swivel chair, crosses her arms, and smiles. "Because you're right about one thing, Will. There isn't room at this school for both of us. And I was here first."

"Well, I'm not leaving," I say. "Just because you're scared of me—"

"Please," she says. "I'm scared of you why, exactly?"

"It's obvious that I'm far better at this than you are. I know how to hack into the computer system, and let's face it: my backstory is way more pathetic than yours. I've got dead parents *and* a radioactive grandma. You're old news around here, but I'm fresh and interesting, and you haven't even seen me play lacrosse yet." The truth is, I've never played lacrosse, but I'm not going to tell *her* that. "You're terrified I'm going to steal all your action."

"Even if I agreed to let you stay," she says, "what makes you think you can fix things with Dr. Melville?"

"Well, for one thing, I know what Dr. Melville looks like" —I turn the computer around again so she can see the school website, featuring a picture of a jovial-looking man with a full gray beard—"and the guy that you sent to my room in the middle of the night definitely wasn't him. Who was he? Just some local rube that you paid to throw on a Connaughton bathrobe and scare me?"

Andrea gets quiet for a really long time. She scrunches her lips together and steeples her fingers, and now the frown across her forehead makes her look like she's concentrating on something very intensely.

"What if . . ." she says, sitting down next to me, "we decide . . . to make it interesting?"

"How so?"

"We both want to stay here at Connaughton, correct? And we both have enough dirt to rat each other out. So what if we agree on a mark, a student here" —she pauses to think—

"somebody who's rich enough to make it worthwhile. The first one to get this individual to fork over, say, ten thousand dollars . . . gets to stay."

I'm already smiling. "And the loser?"

"Packs it in," she says. "Happy trails."

"You're serious?"

"One thing you'll learn about me, Will. I never joke about money. Ever." She looks at me. "So do we have a deal or not?"

"Oh, it's on," I say, barely resisting the urge to add the words *like Donkey Kong,* because I don't want to blow the mood. "But how do we choose the mark?"

And just then, her door bursts open.

FIVE

THE GUY WHO STUMBLES INTO ANDREA'S ROOM IS WEAR-
ing candy-striped boxer shorts, a rumpled bathrobe,
and cowboy boots. His gelled blond hair is sticking
up sideways in the back, and he's got a girl dangling off each
arm. All three of them look as if they've been up all night, and
they all start laughing hysterically when they see Andrea and
me sitting on the bed staring at them.

"Huh," he snorts, stumbling forward until the girl on his
left has to catch him and hold him up. "I guess this *isn't* the
shower. Hey . . ." Leaning forward, he screws his face up into a
squinting, cockeyed stare. "Wait a second. You're that new kid
from Bodkins's class, right? The missionary kid?"

That's when I recognize him—the loud snorer from English Lit. I'm still trying to remember his name when he lets
go of the girls and flounders forward with outstretched arms,
flinging himself across Andrea's room. I'm not sure where he
thinks he's headed, but he ends up in the corner, wrestling
with her cello case.

"I've always wanted to try one of these." He grins, holding
up the case and fumbling with the clasps. "It's like a giant uku-
lele, right?"

"Leave it alone, Brandt," Andrea says, reaching for him,

but he shoves her away and pops open the case. The cello falls out and hits the floor with a twangy crash. Still grinning, the guy grabs it up off the floor. In the doorway, the two girls are shrieking with laughter like this is the funniest thing they've ever seen, as he starts plucking and strumming the strings with his fingers, belting out the Bill Withers classic "Ain't No Sunshine" at the top of his lungs. Strings snap and break.

"Quit it!" Andrea lunges for the cello, but the guy moves at the last second, and—accidentally or on purpose—her hand makes contact with his face with a sharp whack.

All at once, the fun comes to a screeching halt. The guy glares at her, and I can see the red imprint of her hand on his cheek. He picks up the cello by the neck and slams it down onto the floor, then raises one foot and stomps on it with his cowboy boot. It splinters, pieces of polished wood flying in every direction.

"Hey, whoa," I say, rising from the bed, but that's as far as I get before Kid Boxer Shorts swings around and drives his elbow into my stomach, leaving me doubled over and sucking air into parts of my body that I didn't realize even needed oxygen. Already I can tell that it's going to be a while before I can speak in a normal voice. When I manage to straighten up, I see Andrea just standing there, staring at what he's done. Even the girls in the doorway have stopped laughing.

"You like that?" he says. "Huh? Was that good for you?" He glowers at the broken pieces of the cello. "Maybe next time you'll dial it down a little when somebody's just having a laugh, right?"

"Mr. Rush?"

It's a female voice coming from the doorway, and I look up to see that the two girls have vanished and been replaced by a tall, severe-looking house matron standing just outside the room. She's dressed in a black suit and skirt, with iron-colored hair and a sharp, beaklike nose. She looks like she could kick all of our butts. Emily Dickinson meets Angie Dickinson, back in her *Police Woman* days, at least. I've caught the reruns on late-night TV.

"What exactly is going on?" she demands. "What on earth . . ." Her eyes flick to me, then to Andrea, and back to the cello smasher. "What are you doing here?"

"Just having some fun," the guy mumbles, weaving his way to the door so that the woman has to step aside to keep him from crashing into her. Unbelievably, she does just that, allowing him to walk away.

"Mr. Rush," she says again, this time to his back. "I'm sending you to Dr. Melville's office for disciplinary action, right away. And *you*—" She points in my direction. "Male students are not permitted in the female dorms."

"Yes, ma'am," I say. "I was just helping clean up, and I'll leave."

The matron looks at the mess on the floor, obviously created by Brandt, and I can feel her trying to decide whether to ask any more questions. Then, with a pinched-mouth grimace, she nods. "See that you do."

After she leaves, I look back at Andrea. She's bent over, gathering up the broken pieces of her instrument. I get down on my hands and knees to help her, but she pushes me away.

"Just leave it," she says in a toneless voice. Her hair's hanging in her face so I can't see her expression. "Go. Get out of here. Leave me alone."

"He's the one," I say. "It has to be him."

She stops and looks up at me, and I see that her eyes are red. "What?"

"That jerk. He's our mark."

"You're kidding, right?"

"Um . . . no?"

"That's Brandt Rush." Andrea sits up, then slumps back against the wall with her chin on her knees, looking hopeless. "Don't tell me you haven't heard of him."

"Should I have?"

"As in, Rush's?"

"What, you mean the retail empire?" I shrug. "So what? It doesn't give him an excuse to act like a total jerk."

"Will . . ." Andrea just shakes her head. "You still don't get it, do you?"

"I'm new here, remember?"

"Forget it." She stands up. "It doesn't matter," she says. "Go. Now."

I get to my feet and head toward the door, brushing the shards of wood from the knees of my jeans, then stop and look back. "Who were those guys that you sent to my room, anyway? The ones who were supposed to be Melville and the security guard?"

"Just a couple of friends from town." Andrea's still looking down at the remaining pieces of her cello. "They owed me a favor. Why does it matter?"

"So as far as the administration knows, I'm still a student here?"

"Yes," she says, "but I already told you—"

I hold up my hand, stopping her. "Andrea?"

"What?"

"Game on."

And I close the door before she has a chance to answer.

SIX

WHEN I GET BACK TO MY ROOM, THERE'S A NEATLY wrapped bundle sitting outside my door. I pick it up and peel back the tape, peering down at a perfectly folded blazer and dress pants, white shirt, and tie. My uniform has arrived.

I carry it inside along with my backpack. The room is still a mess from last night's hurried departure—my bed is unmade and the half-finished orientation paperwork is scattered across the floor. It feels strange to be back after crawling out the window in the middle of the night, but I'm already starting to get used to the idea of being a student here.

I sit on the bed and take a second to get my thoughts in order. From here, one of two things is going to happen. Either Andrea will rise to the challenge—which was really her idea anyway—or she'll rat me out to the administration for real, in which case I'll have no choice but to leave for good. But I really don't think that's going to happen, because Andrea knows she can't do that without getting herself in trouble. Besides, I saw the look on her face when Brandt smashed her cello.

She wants payback.

While I'm sitting there contemplating the situation, I get a text message from Andrea117 on my phone.

Meet me after English Lit outside the arts center.

I read the text twice before deleting it and making sure it's gone for good. The message means she's either in or at least interested enough to talk through the details. Grabbing my towel, I head down the hall for a shower, mindful of my bruised stomach muscles where Brandt hammered his elbow. When I get back to my room, I try on my uniform for the first time.

The jacket, shirt, and pants fit perfectly. I get the tie right on the first try, then rake my fingers through my hair until it looks halfway presentable. For the moment, the guy staring back at me from the mirror almost looks like he belongs here. I smile. If I can fool myself, then the rest of my classmates should be a breeze.

Five minutes later, armed with my class schedule, I'm speed-walking down to the dining hall for an epic helping of gourmet huevos rancheros with a latte and fresh-squeezed orange juice. The eggs are delicious, light and fluffy, with roast tomato-serrano salsa, corn tortillas, black beans, and fresh cheese, and I manage to polish the whole thing off without getting any on my tie. Meanwhile, it's almost nine o'clock, which means I've got World History 443: Twentieth-Century India and China starting in less than ten minutes. If I hurry, I can make the bell.

I head out of the dining hall, riding on a river of well-dressed, bright-eyed baby billionaires on their way to various training seminars on how to rule the twenty-first-century world. I'm glancing down at the map to make sure I'm headed in the right direction when I see a big group of students up ahead gathered around the statue of Lancelot Connaughton.

Except it's not the statue they're looking at.

There's a student perched on top of Connaughton's shoulders. He's wearing nothing but a ski mask and a pair of red swim trunks, and he's trying to hold perfectly still, like he's part of the statue, but it's cold out here and I can see him shivering. Written across his bare chest in what looks like black marker is a stylized letter *S*. As uncomfortable as it seems, it's pretty obvious that he's actually *choosing* to be up there.

"What is this?" I look at the girl next to me, who's snapping a photo with her iPhone. "What's going on?"

"Hazing ritual," she says.

"For what?"

"The Sigils."

"Who?"

She glances at me. "You're new here, aren't you?"

"Is it that obvious?"

"The Sigils are a secret society on campus. Every year they invite two or three new students to join. Nobody knows who's in it, but the members always make new recruits do something like this to get in."

For a second we both stand there looking up at the poor kid. "How long does he have to stay up there?"

"Till his assignment's over." She shrugs, and then from

behind us I hear a man's voice shouting. "I guess his time's up," the girl says, and I glance around to see two security guards lumbering across the quad, making a beeline for the statue.

"You!" one of them shouts. "Get down from there now!"

The kid in the ski mask jumps off Connaughton's shoulders and hits the ground running at top speed, with the two guards struggling to keep up. The crowd of students cheers him on. Before the guards can reach him, the kid ducks into a nearby building and disappears. A roar of approval goes up from the crowd.

"Looks like he made it," the girl next to me says, and the other students are already starting to disperse, heading to class.

"So, this secret society," I begin. "How long has it been around?"

"Who knows? Some people say that Lancelot Connaughton himself started it as a kind of inner circle. Only the members know who the other members are, or why certain people get invited and others don't. It's all very Skull and Bones."

I've started walking again and am consulting my map when a heavy hand falls on my shoulder.

"Hey, hey, there he is." The voice is grating, intimate, and familiar in a way that makes my skin tighten and slither across my shoulders. "You sure picked a crazy place to end up, didn't you, buddy?"

I turn around slowly and look at the man standing there smiling at me, wearing an ill-fitting navy suit with a laminated VISITOR tag dangling crookedly from a lanyard around his neck. Despite the cheap apparel, he's good-looking for a guy on the verge of forty—a touch of gray at the temples, bright pale-blue eyes, and the kind of two-day stubble you get from sleeping in your car. You might even use the word *charming*. I give back to him the best smile I can muster, which, under the circumstances, ought to win me an Academy Award.

"Hey, Dad."

SEVEN

TOOK ME LONG ENOUGH TO FIND YOU UP HERE," HE SAYS, locking one arm around my shoulder and wrenching it tight enough to hurt. "Looks like you've already landed on your feet, huh?" He ruffles my hair in a way that probably looks fatherly, then gives me an extra little open-handed smack on the back of my skull. "I *missed* you, boy."

"I bet," I say.

"You really left me holding the bag down in Trenton, you know that? Not that it's anything your old man can't handle, but when the authorities dropped by and I realized you'd taken off with the last of our seed money—"

"You weren't exactly in any shape to travel," I remind him.

He scowls and shrugs it off with a happy-go-lucky grin. "Sure, kid, whatever you say—we all make mistakes. All I'm saying is, I just wish you would've told me before you took off. Would've at least given me a fighting chance. Anyway, bygones, right?" He shrugs again. "We're back together again, the old team—that's what matters. Looks like you've already got something pretty swanky set up for yourself too, huh? What's the game?"

"Nothing."

"Right." He laughs. "Your mother and I taught you better

than that." He leans back and, without even breaking stride, his head does that casual kind of swivel that I've seen him do since I was old enough to walk: his saucer-size eyes taking in everything—the manicured campus, the million-dollar buildings, the rich kids with their lives of privilege stretched out in front of them like an endless red carpet of private jets and five-star luxury hotels. "So who's the mark?"

I shake my head. "It's not like that."

"Uh-huh."

"I mean it," I say. "I'm done with all that. I'm going straight. That's why I'm here. I'm sick of that old life. I'm never going back to Trenton."

Dad gives me a long, slit-eyed look, and for a change I can't tell what he's thinking. In the past I always could, back when it was the three of us, him and me and Mom, running the wedding-planner scam out of our apartment on Clinton Avenue. In the early days, Dad said they cleared five thousand a week while pulling a pigeon drop on the weekends. He used to talk about retirement until Mom got sick and things changed.

"Billy-boy," he says. "I think maybe you better give this some thought before you go and do something stupid."

"My name is Will." I start to pull loose from him. "Will Shea. And I'm going to be late for class."

His grip tightens around my neck. "I don't think so."

"Mr. Shea?"

I pause and we both turn around to see a heavyset, bearded man coming toward us, walking a dog. I recognize him from the school website as Dr. Melville, the real Dr. Melville, the head of school. Suddenly his dog lunges at Dad, pulling at his leash and barking like crazy, as if he knows exactly what kind of guy he's dealing with. Score one for the dog.

"Chaucer, heel," Dr. Melville commands, then turns to us with a chuckle. "You'll have to forgive him. I'm afraid thirty-two generations of pure English breeding have convinced him that he's on the hunt."

"Yes, sir." I turn and glance at Dad. "This is . . ."

"Louis Keene." Dad smiles, suddenly all sunshine and lollipops. "I'm Will's uncle." He shakes Dr. Melville's hand and then reaches down to scratch the dog's head. "Nice pooch."

"Thank you." Dr. Melville nods at my dad and then turns to me. "I make it a point to personally welcome all new students to Connaughton, but you're a difficult man to reach, Mr. Shea. We're glad to have you here." He turns to my father. "You must be very proud of your nephew, Mr. Keene."

"Oh, I am," Dad says, beaming. "Will's been like a son to me."

"After what happened to his parents on that island . . ." Dr. Melville shakes his head. "What a tragedy. I don't know if you've heard, Will, but I actually wrote my doctoral thesis about the indigenous people of the Marshall Islands."

"No," I say, and feel my throat start to tighten and go dry. "I didn't . . . know that."

"Oh, yes indeed. That was one of the reasons I was so interested in meeting you. Which island was it that you grew up on? Ebeye?"

"Right."

"I know it well," Dr. Melville continues. "In fact, I did most of my research from that military base on Kwajalein, which, as you know, is only a half mile away by ferry." He scowls upward and then glances at me. "The name of that base slips my mind, though. What was it, again?"

"It was . . ." My chest is beginning to ache and I can feel sweat starting to pop out across my upper lip. For a second the morning sun feels ten times brighter than usual, blinding my eyes. Dr. Melville is staring directly at me now.

"The Reagan Test Site," Dad says with absolute casualness. "Right, Will?"

"That's right, of course." Dr. Melville nods and smiles. "Have you been to Ebeye yourself, Mr. Keene?"

"Just for a few days, right after Will was born," Dad says, taking his time, as if there's nothing he'd rather be doing than standing here discussing a place that he's never even seen with his own eyes. "Beautiful lagoon, lovely area, but terribly over-crowded. The slum of the Pacific, they call it. I always hoped for something better for my favorite nephew. And now, thanks to you fine people"—he reaches out and pats Dr. Melville on the shoulder—"he's going to have it."

"Well, we're certainly delighted to have him," Dr. Melville says, and glances at his watch. "I've got a meeting to attend, but we'll talk later, Will, won't we?"

After Dr. Melville leaves, I feel Dad's arm go tight around my shoulder again, delivering another painful squeeze.

"See how good we are together?" he whispers. "Just like the old days. I *knew* you were gonna pull out that dead-missionary-parents wheeze. Like I can read your mind, right? That's why we're *partners*."

I manage to nod.

"Remember that." His voice darkens, becoming more like the one I remember from after Mom died, a threatening growl with a thin layer of good humor painted over it. "I'm getting a room at the Motel 6 in town, but I'll be in touch soon." Then, with one last look around at the century-old marble buildings, Craftsman-style dorms, and immaculately groomed grounds, he drops his voice to just above a whisper. He's practically rubbing his palms together with anticipation. "This is gonna be good," he murmurs. "Son, we're gonna make a *killing* here."

And like that, he's gone.

EIGHT

AFTER WORLD HISTORY, I'VE GOT ECONOMICS 155: INTROduction to Global Risk. I'm expecting a boring classroom full of half-asleep students guzzling energy drinks while some fossil in his sixties drones on about world markets.

Then I step inside.

The room is massive and packed with big TV screens and kids moving in all directions, shouting and talking and staring up at a mission-control center of gigantic wall-mounted monitors scrolling real-time stock quotes and financial data. Half of them are on their phones while the others are keying in trades. It's the Wall Street of the Great North Woods, and for a second I just stand there taking it all in, trying to figure out where I should go.

"Excuse me." I tap one of the students on the shoulder. "I'm new here and—"

"Hang on," the kid says, not taking his eyes off a screen. Thirty seconds later, he throws one hand into the air. "Yes. Yes!" He pumps both fists, throws his arms around me, and slaps me on the back so hard that I almost cough up my eggs. "Okay, bro, what are you looking for?"

"Mr. Dalton," I say, glancing down at my course schedule. "Is he around?"

He steers me through the mob and points out my instructor, Mr. Dalton, who looks about five years older than I am and turns out to be a former day trader and master of the universe whose name even I recognize — mainly from a semi-successful SEC investigation that very nearly shut down his investment firm. He's talking to Brandt Rush, leaning over his shoulder, coaching Brandt's every move.

Not that Brandt needs it. He seems to be completely in his element, trading commodities and raking in piles of virtual cash with the ease and confidence of a born conquistador. Every buy, every short sale, is accompanied by a fist-bump or a high-five with one of a half-dozen sycophants surrounding him. The fact is, I've never seen anybody so utterly in control of a situation. After the end of one particularly complex trade, Mr. Dalton himself actually gives Brandt a chest-bump.

"What's the big deal?" I ask the kid who brought me to the scene.

"We're all trading with virtual funds," the kid says. "Brandt's the only one whose parents let him use actual cash. He just cleared three million dollars short-selling this biotech start-up."

"Three million *actual* dollars?"

"Yeah."

At one point during class, while I'm sitting in front of a massive six-screen Bloomberg Terminal and trying to learn which of the yellow hot keys represent which market sectors, I look up and see Brandt himself staring at me. For a second I know how a field mouse must feel when the shadow of a hawk passes over him. After a moment Brandt makes his way over, all swagger and sneer.

"Yo. Missionary kid."

I don't take my eyes off the screens in front of me. He taps me on the shoulder.

"I think you're in the wrong class," he says, leaning in close. "Why don't you go get me a coffee or something?"

Now I look at him. For the moment, he seems to have lost interest in all the money changing hands, temporarily distracted by the opportunity for a little midday cruelty.

"You heard me," he says. "Lots of cream, lots of sugar."

As I stand up, something snags me around the ankle and I go sprawling forward. I catch myself in time and see Brandt giving me the slightest smirk as he turns back around to the overhead monitors.

"Better watch your step," the kid whom I'd been talking to earlier says. "He's the king of the jungle in here."

"Right," I say. "Thanks." I make my way out into the hallway, heading for the exit. It's cold outside but I don't mind. I've got English Lit in twenty minutes, and I could use the cooldown time.

Now more than ever, I know that we've picked the right mark.

• • •

Andrea doesn't look happy to see me.

After English Lit—where she wouldn't meet my eye, and I managed to avoid Brandt—I find her waiting outside the arts center, Connaughton's brand-new five-million-dollar performance hall, which has been finished so recently that seedling grass outside the main entrance still looks like green hair plugs. The curved glass and steel construction resembles a renegade escape pod that's crash-landed from Planet iTunes, some ultramodern reality where everything is chrome and sleek and ergonomically designed for maximum coolness.

"So." Standing there for a second, Andrea looks me up and down. "I see you learned how to tie a tie."

"Yeah." I reach up and straighten it, feeling unexpectedly self-conscious. "Does the uniform fit okay?"

She doesn't bother answering, just gestures for me to head inside the arts center. The space is bright and airy and crackling with a kind of no-limits excitement that comes from being young and rich with your whole life ahead of you. From above, vast and unobstructed shafts of sunlight cascade down into the three-story lobby, where students are hanging out, chatting and texting like the casually beautiful citizens of the world that they are. Artistic black-and-white student photos line the walls. I smell fresh coffee and glance up to see the familiar green and white sign. "Wait, you've got a Starbucks in here?"

"Try not to look so shocked," she mumbles. "You've been here twenty-four hours."

I follow her through the lobby toward the coffee shop.

According to Connaughton's website, the arts center is the home for four art galleries, a three-hundred-seat theater, an acting lab, art and architecture studios, a darkroom, a music computer lab, and an orchestra room, not to mention a state-of-the-art recording studio. There are rumors that Foster the People mixed part of their latest album here.

Andrea points me to an empty table in a corner of the café, and we sit down. Somewhere off to my left, a man in a dark suit passes by, and I have a panicky moment when I think it's Dad in the crowd. It would be just like him to follow me here. But I realize it's just an instructor.

Andrea leans in. Her eyes are locked on mine. "What's wrong, Will?"

"Nothing. I'm fine."

"For your sake, I really hope you're a better liar than that."

I shake it off, but something about her eyes, the way she's looking at me, makes it difficult to focus. "I thought I recognized somebody, that's all."

"Like you're being followed? Cops?"

"No, nothing like that."

She doesn't look convinced, and I don't blame her. The truth is, I don't even want to think about what it means that Dad has already found me here, or what he could do to mess up my play with Brandt Rush—not that I have one yet.

Dad *is* a problem. Even if he weren't a gambling addict and constantly in debt to a half-dozen of New Jersey's less patient bookies for the worst run of luck in the history of horseracing,

I got the vibe from him that his drinking is getting out of control again. He's an ever-expanding black hole of misfortune with a chronic habit of sucking in whatever's nearby, and at the moment that includes me.

"Listen," Andrea says, seeming to read my mind. "I've already got three good reasons why conning Brandt Rush is a terrible idea. If you've got somebody gunning for you here, that's just one more argument for calling off this travesty now before you do some damage neither of us can walk away from."

"I told you, I'm fine."

"You're sure?"

"Positive."

"Oh, Will." She rolls her eyes. "You *are* a terrible liar."

I give her my best innocent look. "You said something about three reasons?"

She still doesn't seem to believe me but presses on just the same. "I don't know if you noticed the plaque when we first came in?" she says. "Let's start there."

THE RUSH CENTER FOR DANCE AND PERFORMING ARTS is what the plaque in the lobby turns out to say. And if you take the time to read the small print, you can actually see, for those too dense to grasp what the name means, MADE POSSIBLE BY THE GENEROUS DONATION OF VICTORIA AND HERBERT RUSH.

"It's actually a twenty-six-million-dollar endowment," Andrea tells me as we stand there, "to be paid out over the next ten years. Brandt's father and grandfather both went to Connaughton. They paid not only for this new arts center, but also the refurbished boathouse and athletic field house that's going up in 2017, on the other side of campus. All of which means—"

"They're swimming in cash," I say. "I kind of figured that one out for myself, thanks."

"It means," the voice behind me says, "that they own this school."

When I glance around, I see two men standing behind us. The broad-shouldered one is tall and bald, with a head like a hollow-point bullet, and the other is bearded and bespectacled, wrapped up in about twenty pounds of imitation Savile Row tweed. It takes me about five seconds to recognize them as the two that shook me out of bed last night and sent me running across campus with my backpack slapping against my shoulders.

"Friends of yours?"

"Boys," Andrea says, "you've met Will."

"Yeah." I take a half step back. "At one in the morning."

"No hard feelings," Mr. Tweed says, with a little smile. Behind his specs, his green eyes sparkle like sea glass, and I realize that one of his pupils is cocked in a slightly different direction. "Andrea asked for our help."

"Chuck and Donnie are based out of New York," Andrea says. "They were running a boiler-room scam in Queens, but I met them in Boston last year, glim-dropping out on Commonwealth Avenue."

I take a closer look at Donnie's face. "You've got a glass eye?"

Donnie grins and pops it out so I can see it. I've never run the glim-drop scam myself, but I've heard of it. Essentially you've got a well-dressed one-eyed man who walks into a storefront looking for his missing glass eye, and when nobody can find it, the one-eyed man offers ten thousand dollars for its return. The next day, the accomplice "finds" the eye in the store and announces that he's going to return it, but the shopkeeper —thinking of the reward—offers to buy it from him for a few hundred dollars so he can turn around and clear the 10K for himself, but, of course, he never sees either of our boys again. Like all good cons, it works off the greed and selfishness of the mark. The wheeze is strictly nineteenth century, so old it's new, and afterward, nobody wants to admit he's been hustled by such an obvious ploy, meaning that if these two bozos play it right, they can run this game up and down the same three streets for weeks at a time before somebody calls the cops.

"So what are you doing up here?" I ask.

Chuck and Donnie exchange a glance. "Color tour," Chuck says, deadpan.

"Yeah," says Donnie. "We're leaf peepers."

"The point is," Andrea says, "we can't play Brandt Rush like some garden-variety sucker and then give him the brushoff. He gets away with murder at Connaughton precisely because his family has the whole administration in its pocket, and if he gets the slightest whiff of a scam, we're dead before we start. Which means he can't realize that he's been conned—even after the con is over."

"What's the second reason?" I ask.

"He's smart."

"Yeah," I say. "I got to witness him this morning in my Global Risk class. He seems to know what he's doing."

"That's putting it lightly," Andrea says. "Did he talk to you?"

"We're practically best buds."

"Check his GPA," Andrea says. "He sets the curve in all his classes. Daddy sits on the board of Wall Street's oldest brokerage firms, and believe it or not, Brandt's actually inherited his old man's brains." She glances up at Chuck and Donnie, then back at me. "Not that he would ever admit to it. He's way too busy for academics."

"Doing what," I ask, "training for the stringed-instrument demolition squad?"

Andrea shakes her head. "On weekends, he runs a casino out of his dorm room. It's invitation only, exclusively for upperclassmen. Occasionally he'll allow freshman and sophomore girls" — her face tightens with distaste — "but only if they're good-looking enough to meet his exacting standards."

"Have *you* been there?"

Andrea doesn't answer my question. "It's strictly a Friday-through-Sunday shindig, and of course the administration lets him get away with it. He's got a blackjack table, a roulette wheel, and poker." She pauses. "And he cheats."

"How do you know?"

"Trust me."

"Right," I say. "So what's the third reason?"

Andrea takes in a deep breath and lets it out slowly. "He's *mean,* Will."

"I hadn't noticed."

She shakes her head. "I'm not just talking about what he did to my cello," she says. "He's the most vindictive guy I've ever met." She lowers her voice and leans in close. "Last year, when he was a sophomore, there was a girl here, a senior named Moira McDonald, who turned him down for Homecoming. At the time Brandt just blew it off like it was no big thing, but then the following spring, he must have sneaked a hidden camera into her room. The next morning there were photos of her on Facebook . . ." She closes her eyes and shakes her head. "You can imagine what kind I'm talking about. *Everybody* saw them. Moira was going to be valedictorian. She left school two weeks before graduation in total humiliation." Andrea's staring straight at me now. *"That's* how Brandt Rush treats people he doesn't like."

"Okay." I shake my head. "Now I'm definitely going after him."

"Bad call, Will. Take my word for it."

"So you're backing out of our deal?"

"Wow." Andrea doesn't move for a long time. Then I realize that she's started to smile. "You seriously don't have an ounce of self-preservation in your body, do you?"

"Look." I shrug. "You can do whatever you want, but as far as I'm concerned, a schmuck like that was born with a bull's-eye painted on his back. I'm going to take him down on general principles." I stand up. "And when I do, I'm expecting you to honor your end of the agreement—pull up stakes and leave."

"Let's not get ahead of ourselves," Donnie puts in, and

shoots a glance at Andrea, even though one of his eyes doesn't quite go that way. "What are the terms?"

"Hold on." I turn to look at the two of them. "This is between me and Andrea."

"Andrea's a friend," Chuck says. "We owe her one." He takes a step closer to me. "You got a problem with us helping her out?"

After a second, I shake my head. We're all professionals here, and anyway, it appears that the specifics of this arrangement are just one more aspect over which I have no control. But that's fine. The first hints of an idea have already started to incubate in my mind, and I already know how I'm going to win.

"First one to get him to pay out ten thousand dollars cash," Andrea says.

"That's sucker money," I say, shaking my head. "He'll see through it. Make it fifty K, between now and Thanksgiving break."

"Fifty thousand?"

"What, too rich for your blood?"

She cocks her head. "Please."

"That gives us a month to make our play." I extend my hand. "Are you in or out?"

Andrea smiles a little. Her expression is somewhere between awe and pity. "You're already in way over your head."

She's so right. I *am* in over my head. At least it's nothing new.

I'm still holding out my hand, and Andrea's still smiling as she shakes it.

NINE

IT TURNS OUT GETTING INVITED TO BRANDT RUSH'S ROOM FOR Casino Night isn't nearly as difficult as I expected. All I have to do is act stupid, talk loud, and throw money around like water for the next couple days, and by Friday, my invitation comes looking for me.

It happens when I'm hunched over in a study carrel in Connaughton's McManus Library, trying to cram a week's worth of microeconomics into my skull. Shelves of books line the walls up to the cathedral ceilings, with ladders on wheels running up to the higher fixtures, and long, narrow hallways lead to different alcoves. The smells of old paper, parchment, and leather bindings are everywhere.

"Will Shea?"

I look up. The girl standing in front of me is a bronzed Malibu blonde, with a handful of errant freckles and the attentive smile of someone who's heard interesting things about me and wants to find out if they're true. Her school uniform looks custom-tailored to fit her, as if it's been run through a half-dozen of the most exclusive design houses in Paris and Tokyo while she's still been wearing it. After a second I realize she's one of the girls who was dangling off Brandt's arm when he staggered into Andrea's room the other morning.

"That's me," I say, nodding. "And you are?"

"Mackenzie Osborne?" she says, like it's a question.

I've heard of her. Her dad's a big producer out in L.A. whose movies have made about a billion dollars worldwide. "Are you a friend of Brandt's?"

"You could say that." And she actually giggles. "He sent me by with this." She holds out her hand and I see a single red poker chip, bright and heavy, embossed with the initials BTR.

"Monogrammed poker chips," I say. "Pretty swanky invite."

"I know, right?" She lowers her voice to a whisper, because either she's confiding in me or she's just heard that's what you're supposed to do in a library. "Come by tonight: Crowley House, room two forty-four. The tables open at eleven. And you'll want to bring that chip with you."

"Why's that?"

"It opens doors."

"I'll keep that in mind."

"Good." She looks around at the shelves, sniffing the air, and makes a sour face. "Ugh—how can you stand it in here?"

"What?"

"The smell of all these *books*. It smells like—"

"Knowledge?"

"Yuck," she says, and tosses her hair. "You know, Brandt doesn't invite over many new students like this. Especially *scholarship* cases." And then, cocking her head a little: "You must have really done something to impress him."

I seriously doubt that, but I don't say anything. Up until

now, impressing Brandt Rush has been a simple matter of mailing myself what looked like an enormous envelope of cash—really just a roll of cut-up blank paper with a hundred-dollar bill wrapped around it—and then talking loudly to everybody within earshot about what a stud I am at the blackjack table. Inquiring minds took care of the rest. Introducing a rumor into the Connaughton student body is roughly as difficult as introducing a flu bug into a class of sniffling kindergartners—one sneeze and it's all over. Throughout the past three days, Andrea has kept her distance from me, but I could always sense her presence nearby, eavesdropping while I bragged to whoever would listen about the awesome fake ID that I'd used in Atlantic City last summer, teaching myself to count cards and saving up for my next epic success at the tables.

"Well," Mackenzie says, "hope to see you soon." And with that, she sashays off, no doubt vowing never to darken the door of this terrible place again.

Once she's gone, I try to get back to studying, but I'm too distracted to concentrate, thinking about tonight and how I'm going to play it. After five minutes of futility, I gather up my books and carry them to the student behind the circulation desk, waiting while she checks them out and slides them across the counter to me.

"Due back in two weeks," she says.

"Thanks."

"Not that it's any of my business," she says, still looking at the screen in front of her, "but you might want to sit this one out."

I look at her closely for the first time. She's wearing black-framed glasses with lenses that reflect the screen in front of her, and her dark brown hair is pulled back into a ponytail. Her lips are full and coral-pink, and her eyes gleam bluish gray, slanting just a little. Is she smiling? From this angle I can't tell.

"Excuse me?"

"I don't know you"—she looks up at me, and I feel the intensity of her gaze—"but you *really* don't want to get involved with Casino Night. From what I hear, Brandt only invites people he knows he can fleece at the tables."

I glance back at the carrel where I'd been sitting, halfway across the stacks. "You heard all of that?"

"What can I say?" She points to the sign reading QUIET PLEASE. "Some people don't know how to whisper."

"I'm sorry." I take a step toward the desk, trying to catch her eye. "Have we met?"

"Not yet." At last she glances up from the monitor and extends one hand across the desk, her chipped black finger-nails looking like they might have been painted with a Magic Marker. "Gatsby Haverford."

"Gatsby." It takes me less than a second to muse over what kind of parents would name their daughter after one of American literature's most elegant train wrecks, and then decide I'd rather not ask. "Nice to meet you."

"You too." She nods at her computer, where my information is still up on the screen. "Will Shea. You're the transfer student from the Marshall Islands."

"Is that why you work at the library, so you can blackmail the students with their personal information?"

"I guess I just couldn't resist the glamour of the job."

"You're a student here?"

"A junior," she says. "We're in the same English Lit class. But listen, Will. You seem like a decent-enough guy, so take my advice." She leans across her desk and lowers her voice. "If you're so determined to throw your money away, you should just flush it down the toilet. That way there's at least a chance some of it might come back up."

"Don't take this the wrong way," I say, "but we don't even know each other. Why are you so concerned about me?"

"Maybe I just don't like seeing anyone get taken advantage of."

"It hasn't occurred to you that maybe I'll win?"

"No offense," she says, looking me up and down, "but that seems highly unlikely."

"Why's that?"

"Let's just say that when Brandt's running the tables, the odds are forever in his favor."

"Well," I say, "I appreciate the heads-up, but I'm going to take my chances."

"I figured." Gatsby looks at me from between towers of books with a combination of fascination and pity. "But when you walk back in here tomorrow wearing nothing but a barrel and suspenders, don't say I didn't warn you."

"Well, my barrel's out for dry cleaning, so . . ."

Gatsby taps a few keys on the computer, scribbles a note on a scrap of paper, then stands up and comes around from behind the desk. "Stay here." And before I can say anything, she disappears into the stacks, moving through the deep jungle of the Dewey decimal system with all the confidence and authority of a lioness.

While I wait, I find myself looking down at her workspace, at the half-finished cup of coffee and the cracked first-generation iPhone abandoned so trustingly next to the keyboard. I can hear music playing through the ear buds—it sounds like either punk or techno, with some twangy guitar mixed in—and for a moment I'm tempted to pick them up, just to see what she's been listening to. But I'm glad I don't, because when I turn around, Gatsby's already back with an armload of books.

"What's all this?" I look down at the one on top, an old hardcover that looks like nobody's checked it out in decades, and read the title stamped in gold across the spine: *Tips for Winning Poker*. It's resting on two even dustier tomes—*The Mental Game of Poker* and *How to Win at Cards*.

"Look, I appreciate all this, but—"

"Here." She's already checking out the three books, sweeping them under the bar-code reader along with *A Beginner's Guide to Self-Defense*.

"What's this one for?"

"Just take it," she says, and checks out the last title, which I realize is an ancient edition of Kant's *Critique of Pure Reason*.

"And this one?"

"Transcendental logic." She smiles. "You never know when you'll need it."

"Thanks," I say, shoving all the books into my backpack. "But I think what I really need is a bigger bag."

"Happy reading," she says, then goes back around to the other side of the desk, placing the buds in her ears and checking in books again.

TEN

B Y THE TIME I GET BACK TO MY DORM ROOM, I'VE ALREADY forgotten about the books that Gatsby gave me. Mentally, I'm prepping for tonight, and my mind is so preoccupied that when the dinner hour comes, I have to force myself to eat. Voices around me are excited and laughing, discussing weekend plans. I don't talk to anybody. I keep my head down.

After dinner I go back to my room alone, where I sit on the edge of my bed and stare at the wall, running through hypotheticals in my mind, trying to think of everything that could go wrong tonight and how I'd respond. Making sure I'm ready. Figuring the angles. This is the hardest time for me: the waiting.

Outside in the darkness, the hours drag by, doled out by the occasional distant chime of the bell tower. Sometime around ten o'clock, I remember the library books and get them out. Gatsby's choice of the self-defense book and the Kant don't make any sense at all, but I glance over the poker books, more to satisfy my own curiosity than anything else. As I expected, the strategies are fundamental, most of them so simple and outmoded that they're totally useless. Opening the third book, I find a yellow Post-it stuck inside the front cover. It reads:

Will:

*If you're reading this, it means you haven't written me off
as a total whack job. If you still decide to go tonight, good
luck. And be careful around Brandt. If you haven't figured
it out yet, he cheats.*

—G

I peel the note off and stick it up on the corner of my empty
bookshelf, then look at it for a second. Sometime later, the bell
tower chimes again.

It's time to go.

Students at Connaughton have a strict eleven o'clock curfew
on Fridays, so I check to make sure the coast is clear before
slipping out the window with my jacket buttoned up to my
chin. The temperature's already plunged to what feels like
single digits, and late-October starlight is so sharp that it feels
like I could snap off whole chunks of it and suck on them like
icicles. My breath smokes out behind me as I duck below the
eaves of my building, keeping to the shadows.

Crowley House is only three buildings away, but it still
takes me ten minutes of island hopping to get there, since I'm
trying to avoid stepping out into the open. When I reach the
dorm, I stop outside the door and look in at the tall, red-haired
campus security guard shooting me a look of dead-eyed indif-
ference.

I hold up the poker chip and tap it against the glass, and he
opens the door without a word.

"Thanks." Stepping in, I can't help but notice the guard has a dog-eared paperback propped up next to his stool, along with a styrofoam cup of coffee. The book is Kant's *Critique of Pure Reason*. The guard sees me looking at it and scowls.

"Is there a problem?"

"That book," I say. "It's funny."

"I think you've got the wrong author."

"No, I mean, somebody just recommended it to me."

"Yeah?"

I nod. "How is it?"

He takes a sip of coffee and glances down at the cover. "Well, I can't say I'm crazy about his implicit assertion of transcendental idealism denying the reality of external objects." He flicks his eyes up at me. "I mean, I suppose that you could argue that he refutes it in his discussion that self-consciousness presupposes external objects in space, but I'm not totally convinced." Turning, he sits back down on the stool and regards me coolly. "Now, did you want to keep talking about philosophy, or are you ready to go lose all your money to that joker upstairs?"

"Tough call, but I think I'm ready." For the first time I get a look at his laminated ID badge, which reads MURPHY, GEORGE. "Hey, George?"

His expression turns curious. "What?"

"You know much about him?"

"Kant?"

"Brandt."

At the mention of that name, George's whole face goes

sour. "Put it this way," he says. "I've sat here on this stool long enough to watch punks like you throwing your trust funds into his bank account in exchange for a few minutes of feeling like you're some kind of postpubescent jet set."

"So then how come you help him out like this? Serving as his personal doorman?"

"You're new here, aren't you?"

"My first week."

"Let me fill you in on a little secret. There are only two types of people here at Connaughton—the kind that play along with Brandt Rush and his clan, and the kind that don't last." He takes another sip of coffee. "I happen to need this job. Not that you'd know a whole lot about something like that."

"It might surprise you."

"I doubt that," George grunts, and picks up his book again, disappearing behind it until I turn and start upstairs.

Crowley House is even older than my dorm, but it wears its age well, like the cabin of a vintage luxury yacht. It's eleven twenty as I head down the second-floor hall and realize that I've started walking faster, trying to keep time with my heartbeat. My pulse always speeds up when I'm getting ready to start a con. I used to worry about it, but at the last second I always cool off, so I'm hoping tonight is no different.

My mission this evening is simple: figure out how Brandt is cheating, and cheat better. I've got five of the most popular decks stashed in my pockets—Bicycle, Maverick, Bee, Streamline, and Aviator—matched up with the cards I've heard he's most likely to use. It's actually not particularly important that I don't get caught, and at some point I pretty much want him to know that I'm cheating—just not right away.

After that, things are going to get *really* interesting.

I can already hear the hip-hop music and laughter coming from the corner room. And I wonder, what must it be like to be neighbors with Brandt Rush? Or did the housing office just give him his own wing?

I get my answer when the door opens.

The dorm room is actually three singles with the walls knocked down, creating one spacious suite overlooking the quad below. It's already packed with students, thirty of them at least, gathered around the tables, talking and sipping drinks, savoring the occasion as if they were the European crème de la crème in the golden age of the French Riviera. Some are actually wearing tuxedos, and the girls have on cocktail dresses and heels. I find myself thinking of the Sigils. I'm assuming most of the students here belong. Is there some kind of secret handshake?

Nobody so much as glances up when I walk in. I make my way through the crowd, until I find myself face-to-face with Brandt.

"Yo, bro." Grinning, he grabs my hand and shakes it. "Good to see you. I'm totally stoked you got my invite."

"Thanks." I don't know if I'm more shocked by the warmth of his greeting and its ostensible authenticity or by the fact that somebody actually still uses the word *stoked*. Apparently we've come a long way from him sending me out to get his coffee. *The miracle of money*, I think, and smile. "I wouldn't miss it."

"You get in okay? Any troubles at the door?"

"George let me in," I say. "But I think I interrupted his reading time."

"Yeah, dude's a trip, right? Thinks he's Sophocles or something."

"He never gives you any trouble about curfew?"

"Who, that guy?" Brandt says, and rolls his eyes. "He's lucky to have the job. His son's a student here, and the tuition assistance is the only way he's able to keep the kid out of public school. He does as he's told. Anyway . . ." Brandt grips my elbow and steers me hard to the left. "You want a drink? Bar's over there. Epic Phil can hook you up with the beverage of your choice."

"Great." I follow him over to a long freestanding table full of bottles, where another student—the guy who helped me in our Global Risk class—is making three drinks at once, both arms blurring like an adrenalized octopus above a small forest of crystal stemware. "You know Epic Phil, right?"

"Hey," I say, and the guy stops for a second to stick out his hand, which is cold and slightly damp from the martini shaker. His real name is Philip Van Eyck, but I guess he goes by a different moniker when he's slinging martinis. "How's it going?"

"Epic!" says Epic Phil, which I suppose must be his trademark. "What're you drinking?"

"Hmm." I make a big deal of perusing the selection. "Do you have Pepsi products?"

Phil and Brandt exchange a glance and then they burst out laughing, and Brandt pounds me on the shoulder so hard that I feel my sternum pop. "Good one, bro!" he hoots, and tosses a sidelong glance at Phil. "Get him whatever he wants, on the house. He's my guest tonight." Then he grabs my elbow again and steers me toward a table. "Hope you brought your rabbit's foot with you," he says. "Word around the campfire is that you're a regular five-card stud. What's your game?"

Blackjack is the word on my lips when I turn to approach the table and see the dealer standing behind it, shuffling the cards.

"You already met my girlfriend, right?" Brandt asks, and grins at Andrea. "Take good care of him, huh?"

And Andrea smiles back at Brandt and then at me. "Absolutely."

ELEVEN

I'LL GIVE YOU THIS," I SAY, STANDING IN FRONT OF THE TABLE, close enough to whisper. "You *are* good."

Andrea just keeps smiling, as radiant as the lights on Las Vegas Boulevard, as she shuffles the deck. She's already on to the next thing: dealing in new players on both sides of me as they move in, stacking up chips and tossing crisp piles of twenties across the green velvet. Meanwhile, I'm trying to figure out what it means that she's dealing cards for the guy that we're both supposed to be scamming.

When she doles out my cards, I lean in again and whisper, "It didn't take you long to make your move."

"Turns out Brandt likes to jump right into new relationships," she says. "Who knew?"

"So how long have *you* been dating him, thirty-six hours?"

She smiles. "You play him your way, I'll play him mine."

"My thoughts exactly."

My mom was the one who taught me how to count cards. She'd been dealing blackjack at the Palms when she'd met my dad, and my lessons started back when I was eight years old; I was what you might call homeschooled at the time, so I guess that part counted as math. By the time most boys my age were playing Little League and swapping Pokémon cards, I was already dragging in massive pots in basement games against disgruntled, chain-smoking weekend warriors while my dad sat behind me in case anybody got irritated about losing his grocery money to a kid whose voice hadn't even changed yet. People occasionally used words like "prodigy." And "phenomenon." And "cheat."

When Andrea turns back to me now, I flick a fresh hundred-dollar bill onto the table like it's the first one of a long night, even though it represents slightly more than a tenth of my current life savings. And just like that, I'm in the game, counting cards without really realizing what I'm doing. Even out of practice, I'm still quick enough that I can do it while holding up my end of the conversation.

And I win.

And win.

And keep winning.

Normally I'd take it easy, but I'm trying to get Brandt's attention, and in a situation like this, there's only one way to go about it. Nine hands in, I'm up a little more than six hundred dollars and feeling confident enough to slip some of my own cards into my hand, at which point even Andrea can't ignore me anymore.

"What are you *doing?*" she hisses.

"I guess I could ask you the same question," I say. "In fact, I'm pretty sure I did."

"He's already *watching* you. He knows you're cheating."

"Good. I want him to." But before I can say anything else, Brandt drifts over, his joviality just slightly more affected than it had been.

"Yo, Willpower," he says, slapping me on the back. "Looks like you're killing it over here, huh?"

"What can I say?" I shrug. "Beginner's luck."

"Sure. You think maybe you want to pace yourself, give somebody else a chance?"

"Hey," I say. "The way that I look at it, if you can't take the heat, you shouldn't be running a place like this, right?"

Brandt looks like he's just swallowed one of his dad's golf balls, and then he just grins. "Uh-huh." He shoots a glance at Andrea. "Why don't you take a breather, Dre?"

Andrea shrugs, then wraps herself around him for a long, slow kiss, then moves back when another girl steps in to deal. Right away I recognize the newbie—it's Mackenzie, the blond L.A.-producer's daughter who delivered my poker chip to the library.

"Wow," she says. "Guess you remembered your lucky rabbit's foot, huh?"

"Something like that." Turning, I look over to where Brandt and Andrea are laughing with some other kids at the roulette table. "So how long have they been going out?"

"Three days." Mackenzie glances up at me, this time in open amusement. "You're not jealous, are you?"

"Oh, man." I make a disappointed face, like she's caught me in the act. "Is it that obvious?"

"She's not his type," she says, and shuffles the deck.

"Besides, I heard she totally threw herself at him." When Mackenzie deals the next hand, I can feel somebody standing behind me and figure that Brandt's got a spotter sending signals to Mackenzie about my hand. Sure enough, when I glance over my shoulder, there's my good buddy Epic Phil with a big grin on his face, passing me a glass.

"Pepsi?"

"Thanks," I say, but when I reach for it, my hand slips, spilling soda across the floor. "Oh, dude, I'm sorry." By the time Phil's down on his knees soaking up the mess, I've switched out my hand with two other cards. I go big in that round and drag in another hundred and sixty dollars.

Two hands later, I'm up another three hundred and ready to collar up. It's well past midnight, and when Mackenzie stacks up eleven hundred-dollar bills and three twenties in front of me, I can feel Brandt glaring at my back with a kind of radioactive intensity that nobody in the room is going to miss. Even Andrea looks interested in what's going to happen next.

I walk right up to Brandt. "Thanks for inviting me. Anytime you feel like handing free money away, just let me know. I'm always happy to take it."

His mouth tightens. His face is red, and I can see veins standing out in his temples. Self-control isn't a natural state for guys worth as much as he is, and he's barely keeping it together —picture a ten-thousand-piece jigsaw puzzle with an M-80 firecracker sizzling away underneath it. I'm turning away when Brandt grabs my elbow, hard, yanking me close enough to speak into my ear.

"How'd you do it?" he snarls.

"Easy." I shrug. "I'm just a better cheater than you are."

"So you don't deny it?"

"Actually, I pretty much just confessed."

"How? Counting cards?"

"A magician never tells his secrets," I say. "It spoils the trick."

"How come none of my dealers spotted it?"

"Maybe you should consider using smarter people." I glance around the room. "I hear it's supposed to be a pretty good school."

He loosens his grip slightly and actually seems to consider what I said for about half a second. "If you cheated, then I guess you won't mind paying me back what you took."

"Sure." I pull out the wad and fork it over—easy come, easy go—and watch him make a big show out of counting the cash, although what he's really doing is deciding how furious to let himself get, being humiliated like this in his own place. The answer comes a split second later when he nods at a great swaggering glandular catastrophe of a kid—six foot three with close-cropped red hair and shoulders the size of former Soviet republics—who grabs me by the shirt, swings me around, and slams me up against the door hard enough to knock me through it, out into the hallway. I hit the floor, landing on my tailbone under a fire extinguisher. My arms go numb right down to my fingertips. On the un-fun-o-meter, it's right up there next to dental surgery.

When I look up, Brandt and his pet mutant have stepped

into the hall and are looking down at me. The guy's got a lacrosse stick pointed at my face, so close that I can smell the grass stains.

"Give me one good reason why I shouldn't have Carl use your face as a punching bag," Brandt says coolly.

"Well, for one thing," I say, "that's a lacrosse stick, and you wouldn't want to mix sports metaphors. And secondly . . ." I manage to get up, although it takes some time, and start rubbing the feeling back into my butt. "I'm not here on my own."

"What?"

"See for yourself." Digging into my back pocket, I whip out a sheet of paper with my photo and real name on it—my profile page from the New Jersey Department of Human Services —and toss it to him. "I'm not even really a student here. It's all a scam."

"What . . . ?" Brandt stares at the printout for a long time. Knots of muscle bulge in his jaw, and he cocks his head to one side, frowning. "You've got thirty seconds to explain yourself."

"My boss sent me in here tonight to soak you for as much as I could get."

"Who's your boss?"

"Brian McDonald. He runs a crooked online poker game north of Boston. Mentioned settling a score with you over something you did to his daughter last year, a girl named Moira?"

Brandt shakes his head. "I don't know any . . ." he starts to say, and then he stops. "Wait a second—Moira McDonald?" His whole face changes, and his eyes look like they're about to pop right out of his skull. "What about her?"

"I don't know. He just sent me to burn you—that's it. Paid me a hundred bucks plus whatever I could win."

"I guess you failed," Brandt says, and nods at Carl, who hauls off with the lacrosse stick and whacks me in the face. It feels like somebody set off a cherry bomb in my jaw, and that turns out to be the best of it—when my skull slams against the wall, I don't see just stars, I glimpse whole galaxies and nebulae erupting beneath my eyelids. From somewhere in the distance I hear Brandt say, "Break his nose," and I'm aware of Carl getting ready to swing again.

"Wait." I throw my hands up, just in time. "Hold on."

Brandt gives me a look. "What?"

"I can't go to Mr. McDonald like this. You already took your money back. If I return with a broken nose, he'll never use me again."

Brandt smirks. "Then I guess you should've picked a different guy to work for, huh?"

"I wish it were that simple." I shake my head. "If it weren't for that two million . . ." And I start slinking back down the hall toward the stairway.

"Wait a second," Brandt says behind me. "What did you just say?"

I turn around. "You think I like working for a guy like McDonald? You think I'd go through all of this for a lousy hundred bucks?"

"You said two million."

"McDonald's a bully and a creep. The guy's issues have issues."

"You said two million," Brandt repeats.

"Okay. Here's the truth." I glance down at my feet. "The only reason I'm still working for McDonald is because I know his online poker operation backward and forward. I've studied his process, I've seen how everything works, I've got friends on the inside"—and now I stare right at Brandt, directly into his eyes, dropping my voice to a whisper—"and I'm going to take him for all he's got. Which is about two million." I pause for dramatic effect. "You want in, you let me know. All you gotta do is meet him. You'd see."

Brandt stares back at me coolly, his expression unreadable. "That's a whole lot of risk to take just because somebody's a bully and a creep."

"Yeah, well," I say, and now it's time to sell it. "He dated my mom for a while and got rough with her. Knocked her around a time or two. The last time, he broke her jaw." I narrow my eyes. "That's when I decided to go to work for him."

"Taking matters into your own hands, huh?"

"Let's just say it's personal with me."

"You're breaking my heart." Brandt snorts and rolls his eyes. "You think I want to hear your life story?" he asks, but I can tell that something in his face has relaxed, and even though he doesn't know it himself, I can tell that he's beginning to trust me.

Which is how I know I've hooked him.

TWELVE

WHAT HAPPENED TO YOUR FACE?" DAD ASKS.
It's Sunday morning, and I'm sitting on a lumpy mattress in the two-hundred-dollar-a-week room that he's got at the Motel 6 in town, twelve miles from Connaughton, while he finishes shaving. The bathroom door is open just wide enough that I can see his half-lathered face in the mirror, his eyes reflected back on me, our conversation punctuated by the occasional *clink-clink-clink* as he taps the whiskers from the razor into the bathroom sink. The room smells like stale bourbon, dirty laundry, and somebody else's cheap perfume. Put them all together and you've got a scratch-and-sniff Father's Day card that basically comprises my entire childhood.

"Mind if I open a window?"

"Are you kidding?" He steps out of the bathroom, toweling off. "It's twenty degrees out there."

"Yeah, well, I can barely breathe in here."

"Don't change the subject." Crossing the room, he picks up the Cumberland Farms coffee that I brought him, peels off the plastic lid, and takes a big gulp. "I thought you were living large over at that fancy school of yours. But you don't return any of my phone calls all week, and now all of a sudden you show up looking like somebody's been using your face for a catcher's mitt. What gives?"

I take a deep breath. The next four words are going to be painful, but there's no sense in delaying the inevitable. "I need your help."

He grins. "At last, the boy sees reason. What's the play?"

"I want to run the online poker con."

"The online . . ." Dad stops smiling. He puts the coffee down, and his freshly shaved face now looks pale and hung-over. "That's suicide, kid. You trying to get clipped?"

"You haven't even heard my angle yet."

He shakes his head. "Don't need to."

"It's a solid grift."

"I know it's a solid grift, boy. I invented it."

He's wrong, but right now I don't see any reason to argue the point. The online poker swindle is a modern-day twist on the prehistoric wire con that guys like us have been running since the invention of money.

Here's how it works: You tell the mark about your boss, some shady character who runs an online gambling business out of a rundown office space. The specific type of gambling doesn't really matter—it can be poker, blackjack, the ponies, whatever. You bring the mark by, in person, to see how the whole thing works and then tell him you've figured out a way to beat the system—all you need is a guy on the outside to place the bets. Naturally the mark is going to be suspicious of this, so you prove your trustworthiness by fronting him the money and letting him win a few small bets—a thousand here, a thousand there. Once he starts winning, the small potatoes don't satisfy him anymore and he slaps down a huge bet with his own cash, a big enough buy-in that winning is going to bring the whole place down around your boss's ankles.

And that's when we all suddenly disappear, along with the mark's money.

For a guy like Brandt, I'm thinking two million isn't too much to expect.

Dad listens to everything I'm saying without adding a word. Finally he goes to the closet, takes a shirt off a hanger, sniffs the pits, and slips it on. "That scam got us clipped down in Trenton, in case you forgot. What makes you think it'll work any better here?"

"We didn't go wide enough with it in Trenton," I tell him.

Dad sighs. "Kid, you tax me. You really do." He rubs one freshly shaved cheek. "Who's the mark?"

And I tell him about Brandt Rush.

"Two *million?* Seriously?"

That's how I know he's interested, because he's already sitting at the wobbly, cigarette-marred table in the corner of the cheap hotel room, his coffee forgotten, while he works out the figures in his small, careful handwriting. "If he's that rich already, what makes you think he'll go for it?"

I hold up two fingers. "One, he's greedy, and two, he holds a grudge. This is a guy who's still creased that Moira McDonald turned him down for Homecoming last year, and he got twice as creased when I told him that her father sent me in to cheat him in his own casino. He's ripe for the plucking."

Dad thinks about that for a long time, looking down at the numbers he's been adding up and then back at me.

"If we do it—and I'm saying *if*—we'd need a base of operations, computers, office furniture, and at least six guys who look like they know what they're doing . . ." His gaze drifts slightly off to the right as he considers the necessary components of a swindle this size. "They'll have to work on percentage. I don't know if I can swing that."

"I was thinking I could talk to Uncle Roy," I say.

Dad grimaces but doesn't argue, tipping me off that he'd already been thinking the same thing. For him, going to Mom's side of the family for money is kind of like walking into a Boston sports bar wearing a Yankees cap. But if we need operating cash, Uncle Roy might be our only option.

"How soon does it need to be set up?" he asks.

"That's the wrinkle." I sit down across from him. "I need to pull the whole caper off before Thanksgiving."

"Four weeks?" Dad scowls. "That's nowhere near enough time to set the hook and make our play."

"It's going to have to be."

"What's your hurry?"

I don't say anything.

"You might as well tell me, kid. I'm gonna find out anyway."

"It's nothing," I say. "I just don't want this dragging on too long, that's all. It's too much exposure."

Dad just squints at me. He's about to say something when there's a knock. We both stand up immediately, our old instincts instantly activated, and I duck into the bathroom as he crosses the room to the door, careful to keep away from the window. "Hello? Who's there?"

"Who do you think, silly?" a woman's voice asks from outside.

I hear the lock disengage and the rattle of a chain.

"Hey, baby," Dad says casually, in a voice that curdles the acid in my stomach. I've left the bathroom door open a crack, and I can see a woman step inside the room. She's dyed blond, probably in her late thirties but with that finely wrinkled tiredness around the eyes that comes from hours spent at the end of a bar with a cigarette in her hand, getting guys like my dad to buy her drinks.

"I forgot my scarf here," she says. "I thought I'd come back and see if you were still around."

"My loss," Dad says. "I was just heading out for the morning."

"You want company?"

"Wish I could. It's kind of a business breakfast."

"On *Sunday*?"

"The Lord's business won't wait." Dad gives her a smile, his voice oozing charm. "I need to be alone this morning. How about I call you this afternoon?"

"You didn't seem to mind me so much last night," the woman says, pouting.

"That's because he was drunk," I say, stepping out of the

bathroom to make my presence here known. The woman kind of gapes at me, and I just look back at her. It makes me think of the line from that old Rod Stewart song: *The morning sun when it's in your face really shows your age.*

Dad doesn't miss a beat. "Rhonda, this is my son, Billy, the one I told you was a student at Connaughton. Billy, meet Rhonda."

I stay where I am while she glances at my father, then back at me. For a second the only sound is a TV playing in another room. Canned laughter.

"You found your scarf," I say. "Was there anything else you needed?"

Rhonda opens her mouth and then quickly snaps it closed, hard enough that I can almost hear her lipstick flaking off. My father slips an arm over her shoulder and ushers her out the door, murmuring something reassuring about calling her later. He shuts the door behind her, then spins back to me, his arm shooting out to grab me by the collar, yanking me toward him.

"What was that?" he says sharply.

"Funny," I say. "I was going to ask you the same question."

Dad leans in until I can count the veins on his nose. "Listen, you snot-nose little punk. You might think you're some big noise up here in the middle of nowhere, setting up a scam for this Rush kid. But if you start getting delusions of grandeur, you're gonna end up face-down in the dirt before you even know what's hit you." He shakes me hard enough to rattle my teeth. "Are we clear?"

"Let me go," I say, jerking myself free, and somewhere underneath my pounding heart, I can feel that old familiar thickening in my throat, the hot, salty heaviness of unspoken anger rising up in my eyes. It's weakness, and I hate myself for feeling it, but I can't make it stop. "Why do you always have to do that?"

He glares at me with disgust. "I didn't even grab you that hard."

"That's not what I'm talking about." I glance at the door and try to ignore the stench of cheap perfume, but it's so strong now that it makes me want to puke. "Mom wasn't like that."

"No," he says. "She wasn't."

"Then why do you always do this?"

Dad sits down on the side of the bed and rubs his face with his hands. He doesn't seem to know what to say, and for once it's actually comforting. Finally he looks up, stretching out his cheeks as he glances at me, and draws in a deep breath. "Billy . . ."

"Forget it," I say, and head for the door. "I'm leaving."

"Just hang on, kid, okay?"

"I've got homework," I say, not looking back. "I'll call you after I talk to Uncle Roy."

And I step out into the cold air, where my lungs start to loosen and I'm finally able to breathe again.

THIRTEEN

ON THE BUS BACK TO CONNAUGHTON, I TRY TO PUT MY thoughts together again. I don't want to think about any of what just happened, but I know if I don't, it'll all keep festering in the back of my mind—Dad, the empty bottles in the motel wastebasket, and the women like Rhonda who appear to be drawn to him no matter where he goes. Dad has a penchant for the women who seem least like the woman I remember as my mother. I wish I could hate him for it, but instead it just makes me feel sick and sad. Involving him in all of this was a necessary evil, so in the end I start thinking only of the specifics of the con, to try to keep my thoughts off the uglier aspects of it.

As I get off the bus, the cold wind slaps me in the face and cuts right through my jacket. The whole campus feels empty and desolate, and without knowing where I'm headed, I find myself stepping inside the library.

The stacks are even quieter than usual, almost empty, and I see Gatsby behind the circulation desk, again surrounded by towers of books to be checked in.

"Hey," I say.

She glances up at me from between two piles. "Oh, hey, Will." Then she frowns. "What happened to your face?"

"I'm fine. I just fell down some stairs."

"And landed on your *face?*"

"Crazy, I know. Do you have any books about gravity?"

She gives me a sympathetic smile. "You didn't read that one I gave you on self-defense, did you?"

"No, but I'm seriously thinking of reading Immanuel Kant," I say, and seeing her knowing expression, I realize that what happened with the security guard could not have been mere coincidence. "How did you know about George?"

"Who's George?"

"The security guard who let me in. He was reading that same book by Kant."

"Well, you know, everybody reads Kant." She gives me an innocent look. "He's like the J. K. Rowling of western philosophy, right?"

"Uh-huh," I say, and wait for the truth. Finally she sighs.

"Okay," she says. "I grew up in a used bookstore. Wherever I go, I can't help noticing what people are reading. I know George is Brandt's personal doorman on Friday nights, and when I saw he was reading Kant, I figured it wouldn't hurt for you to have something to make small talk about." She looks at me curiously. "Did it work?"

"Not exactly."

"How did the gambling go?"

"As expected."

"So that's good?"

"More or less." I glance at the desk, where Gatsby's own

notebooks and course materials are mixed in with the library books that she's cataloging. "How's work?"

"Slow," she says. "But that's fine with me. I'm just trying to finish that Hawthorne paper for Bodkins's class. How's yours coming along?"

"Bodkins?" I say, and think: *Oh no.*

"Will, are you *serious?*" Gatsby gives me an incredulous look. "You forgot about it, didn't you?"

"It's okay. I do my best work under pressure."

"I bet you do." She looks at me for a long moment and seems to decide something. "You want to see something?"

"Sure."

"Okay." She flips a little library sign around so that it reads BACK IN FIVE MINUTES and grabs a set of keys from beneath the desk. "Follow me."

I trail her across the reading room and through a door in the back, then up two rickety flights of wooden stairs. It's drafty back here, almost as cold as it is outside. The landing at the top takes us to a long, narrow corridor that seems to stretch on forever, past darkened rooms full of dimly lit shelves.

"Where are we now?"

"This place is huge," she says. "Apparently there are whole levels of this building that nobody ever goes to anymore. I've heard that hidden somewhere there's actually a secret library within the library."

"What's in there?"

"Contraband books. Arcane compendiums of forbidden lore."

"Like vegan cooking?"

"Like the basement of the Vatican." At the far end of the hallway is another door, and Gatsby unlocks it and pushes it open. "Watch your step."

We make our way inside, into darkness. It smells different in here—not dusty, but still very old. As she switches on the lights, I realize that we're standing in an open rotunda looking down into a huge circular room. It's climate-controlled with special receded track lighting, shining down on different glass cases as in a private museum—a Batcave for bibliophiles.

"Whoa," I say. "What is this?"

"The rare books collection." As we enter the main room, I look into one of the cases and see that it's full of life-size paintings of birds, a riot of bright colors. "That's Audubon's *Birds of America*," Gatsby says. "An original edition from the 1820s. They printed them on the biggest paper they could find at the time, what they called double elephant folios."

"What're they worth?"

"This particular volume?" She thinks for a moment. "I'm not exactly sure. It's not complete, but then again, almost none of Audubons are, since the original plates were sold individually to subscribers. Still, Connaughton's got the most comprehensive collection this side of the New York Public Library."

"How do you know so much about books? You really grew up in a used bookstore?"

"Yeah. It was my parents', so I worked there growing up.

We lived on Martha's Vineyard. The store went out of business a few years back, but I spent my childhood in an old barn, sorting through boxes of old hardcovers. Occasionally I'd find a treasure."

"The Vineyard, huh?"

She nods. "So I guess that means we both grew up on islands."

"I'm pretty sure the president never vacationed on mine." I'm walking toward the largest case, in the very center of the room. "Is this what I think it is?"

"That's it."

She's joined me. We're both standing at the case with our heads almost touching, looking down through the glass at the oversize illuminated pages of what can only be an original Gutenberg Bible.

Gatsby glances up and whispers: "Do you want to touch it?"

I stare at her. "Are you serious?"

"Here." She pulls a pair of latex gloves from a box beneath the case and hands them to me. "Put these on." Then she crosses the room to a console on the far wall and taps in a quick series of digits.

"What are you doing?"

"Overriding the alarm."

I stare at her, aware of a rising swarm-of-bees sensation in my stomach, which is expanding to fill my chest. "You've done this before, haven't you?"

"Once or twice." After walking back over to where I'm

standing, she slides a key into the bottom of the case and I hear a single, muted click followed by the faintest sigh of released air. Raising the lid, she reaches down and lifts the Gutenberg from its display pedestal. "Sometimes when I'm feeling depressed, I come down here and hold it."

"Is it heavy?"

"See for yourself," she says, and hands it to me.

"Whoa." The book fills my arms with surprising weight. "You know, it's funny—when I woke up this morning I never thought I'd be holding a five-hundred-year-old Bible."

"Connaughton acquired this particular one thirty years ago from a private collector in the U.K.," she says.

"It's beautiful."

"The workmanship is exquisite." Gatsby reaches down and runs her black fingertip along the two long columns of Latin script. "There are only forty-eight known Gutenbergs remaining in the world. All the originals were printed on high-quality linen paper imported from Caselle in Piedmont, northern Italy. It was one of the most important centers for papermaking in the fifteenth century. Every page had an authenticating watermark—either an ox head or a bunch of grapes."

"Huh." I stare at the pages for a long time. "That's weird."

"What?"

"The watermarks." Squinting, I hold the book up to the light, angling it this way and that, and turn the page. "This page doesn't have either one."

"You just need to look closer." Gatsby leans over my shoulder until I can feel her hair tickling my neck. She doesn't say anything for a second. Holding the Gutenberg between us, we turn the heavy pages together, the heavy, brittle paper rustling like autumn leaves. The room falls very still. When Gatsby speaks again, her voice is slow, almost a whisper.

"You're right," she says. "There's no watermark."

"So at least part of this edition is . . ."

She looks at me. Nods. "A forgery."

"Whoa," I say. "I can't believe the school bought a fake." Given the amount of money and prestige at stake, I'm impressed that somebody managed to pull off a bogus sale. Come to think of it, I wouldn't mind talking a little shop with the counterfeit dealers. "Do you think Dr. Melville knows?"

"The whole thing might not be a forgery. Maybe there were just some missing pages and they got replaced with duplicates. Still, that means it's not completely authentic."

"Crazy." I glance around the room, and now I'm wondering how many of these other priceless books might contain forged pages.

"Come on." Gatsby reaches over to take the Gutenberg from my arms. "We should lock this back up again before somebody finds us down here."

Five minutes later we're back at the circulation desk, out of breath and trying to act casual while Gatsby takes a seat behind her computer and starts checking in books. "Stop looking at me like that," she says.

"Like what?"

"Like we just did something illegal."

"We didn't," I say. "I just haven't had this much fun in a library since . . . well, ever."

"*Fun?*" She picks up a book and slides it under the bar-code reader with trembling hands. "We just discovered that the crown jewel of Connaughton's rare books collection is a forgery."

"Well, anything that starts out with overriding an alarm system can't be all bad."

Gatsby just looks at me. "I still can't believe it. It's incredible."

"I know."

"It just never occurred to me that it could be a fake," she says. "How could anyone do something like that?"

"Yeah, I know." The truth is that people like me are always trying to figure out a way to fake something and pass it off as real—rare books, business contracts, deeds to nonexistent real estate. "People will surprise you, I guess."

She glances at the phone on her desk. "We have to tell somebody."

"Like who, the library police?" I shake my head. "I think maybe for right now we should keep this to ourselves until—"

"Hey, bro. Where you been?"

I stop midsentence and look around to see Brandt standing there with Andrea on his arm. For a second, he just glowers at me, and then his face breaks into his easy-like-Sunday-morning grin. Andrea is already smiling, bright-eyed and cute as a button above her scarf, her cheeks apple-red from the chill of the day. Brandt slams me on the shoulder with a bone-jarring *thwack.*

"How's it going?" He leans down, voice dropping to a whisper. "Glad to run into you here. I wanted to talk to you about that opportunity you mentioned the other night. When can we go see this boss of yours?"

In the moment of silence that follows, I can feel Gatsby's questioning eyes on me. "Actually"—I turn to flick a glance at Andrea, hoping my reaction comes off as looking nervous enough—"I'm not really sure if I can still—"

"Friday night is Homecoming," Brandt says. "I won't be running the casino that night. We'll go together to talk to him then."

"What about the dance?" Andrea asks.

"I'll put in an appearance and be out of there by eight." He looks at me again. "Make it happen, okay?" His voice tightens. "Don't waste my time." He turns to Andrea, who's pretending to look at the books on the circulation desk. "You ready, babe?"

"I'm always ready . . . babe," Andrea murmurs, and leans in to kiss him with enough visible tongue that Gatsby and I are basically forced to pretend we're someplace far enough away that we can't hear the sucking noises they're making. We're talking feeding time at the aquarium. I don't even want to know what Andrea has to think about in order to sell it.

"I'll see you around," I say, nodding toward Gatsby, and walk away. The last thing I see is Andrea's face smiling smugly at me as I head out the door.

FOURTEEN

I T'S STILL DARK OUTSIDE WHEN MY CELL PHONE GOES OFF ON Monday morning with a 702 area code—Las Vegas. It's five a.m. here, which means that where Uncle Roy is calling from it's not even early—it's still late.

"Hey, Uncle Roy," I croak, shaking off the cobwebs while I scan the floor for an unopened bottle of Mountain Dew to pour over my brain and wake it up.

"William!" Roy's voice bellows, and I can hear the endless ringing of slot machines and the rabble of voices in the background. "Did I catch you sleeping?"

"No," I say, "I was just getting up."

Roy is my mom's uncle, making him my great-uncle and the single greatest old-school-confidence man that I know. For most of his life, he's lived in Vegas, working security before he became a full-time grifter like his favorite niece. Back when the old MGM Grand burned down in 1980, he was part of the retrieval team that the casino sent into the vault to get the money out, while the place was still smoldering. He and a handful of other guards carried the cash to a secret location to await pickup from an armored car. He used to tell me stories of hauling pillowcases stuffed with bills past the scorched bodies of gamblers who were melted to slot machines because they hadn't been able to walk away, even while the place went up in flames. At eighty-two, Uncle Roy is one of the toughest guys I've ever met, and he still hasn't gotten over Mom's death.

"Sorry I haven't had a chance to call you back, William," Roy says. "I've been a little busy."

"I thought you were taking it easy these days," I say.

"Yeah, I've never worked harder than after I retired," Roy says, chuckling, and I can hear the faint metallic *snick* of his lighter as he fires up what I'm sure is his twentieth cigarette of the night. "Where are you, anyway?"

"New England," I say. "North of Boston. A prep school called Connaughton."

"Posh digs," he says admiringly. "So what can I do for you? Judging from the message you left, I'm guessing you're looking for funding?"

Good old Roy, never one to waste time. "Well, actually, I'm setting up a little con here," I say, "and I was hoping I could hit you up for some seed money. And maybe a few guys in the Boston area that you could recommend?"

Roy bellows out smoky laughter. "Like mother, like son, huh?" The laughter becomes a wheezing cough, and I wait while it dies away and he gets his breath back. "Sure, I got friends in that neck of the woods. Some of them even owe me a favor. How many guys do you need?"

"Six."

"No problem. What type are you looking for? Distinguished? Continental? Harvard Yard types?"

"Actually," I say, "I'm hoping for some younger faces. Programmers. Silicon Valley by way of MIT."

"Interesting," he says, and I can hear him clicking buttons on a keyboard while an infinitely more complex array of switches and sprockets start turning in his mind. "Yeah, I can think of five guys right off the top of my head that I can get up there by tomorrow. What's the angle?"

"I'm running the online poker swindle on a mark here, a rich jerk sitting on a trust fund the size of Mount Everest. But in order to make it work, I need a full boiler-room setup with computers and phone lines. And . . ." I pause and swallow hard. "I kind of need it by Friday."

"Friday? *This* Friday?" There's a long pause, and I realize Uncle Roy is laughing. "You don't ask for much, do you?"

"Sorry," I say. "You know I wouldn't ask if I didn't really need it."

"Same old William, God love you." He chortles. "Hey, remember back when you soaked that entertainment lawyer for sixteen grand in Reno? You weren't even ten years old at the time." His voice practically glows with fond recollection. "Geez, kiddo, your mom would be so proud."

"Thanks," I say.

"I'll be on the first flight out tomorrow morning."

"Wait." At first I think I've misheard him. "What?"

"My grand-nephew losing his cherry in the big con—you think I'd miss this for the world?"

"Uhhh," I mumble. It's all I say, but when it comes to somebody as intuitive as Uncle Roy, it's one "uhhh" too many.

When Roy speaks again, all the laughter has disappeared from his voice, replaced by a suffocating vacuum of suspicion.

"Your old man's involved in this, isn't he?" he asks.

"Well . . ." I can't lie to Uncle Roy. Even if I could, he'd know it in a second. "Kind of. But it wasn't his idea. I had to bring him in on the deal."

"*William . . .*" Uncle Roy groans. It comes out sounding like a growl, as if I'd just awakened a sleeping bear midway through hibernation. "Why'd you go and do that, kiddo? You know you can always come to me for help. Why'd you have to bring that dirtbag into it?" Uncle Roy has never liked Dad, even back before Mom died, and things have only gone downhill since then. "Is he on the sauce again?"

"Not that much."

"Is he on the lam from somebody?"

"I don't know." At least this much is true. In Roy's mind, Dad has always been the worst kind of grifter, careless and greedy, which makes him a walking occupational hazard. It helps explain why Dad spent the first part of my life in and out of prison, while Roy's never seen the inside of a jail cell. "You think I should cut him loose?"

"Too late now, kid." Roy sighs. "If you drop him now, he'll queer the pitch. What's the nearest airport to you?"

"Manchester," I say.

"Then I'll see you tomorrow."

"You're still in?"

"Somebody's gotta keep your interests at heart," my great-uncle says, and like that, he's gone.

FIFTEEN

FTER UNCLE ROY HANGS UP, I DECIDE TO LIE BACK DOWN for five more minutes of sleep. The next thing I know, it's eleven o'clock (I guess the fancy-schmancy Connaughton blackout curtains really work). I've already missed World History and Economics, and the dimly functioning part of my brain manages to realize that I'm going to be late for English Lit, even if I could somehow magically teleport myself fully dressed to Mr. Bodkins's classroom.

"Crap!" I jump out of bed, throwing on clothes and grabbing my backpack, then run across the already deserted quad and trying to come up with an excuse for my tardiness. My mind is a blank. It's probably ironic that I have no trouble fleecing somebody like Brandt Rush for untold hundreds of thousands or more while I still can't make up a decent story to explain why I'm late to English class, but right now I'm too stressed out to appreciate the distinction.

Ducking into the deadly silence of Mr. Bodkins's class, I'm instantly aware of the eyes of the entire class leveling themselves on me. Mr. Bodkins is hunched, red-eyed, and disheveled behind his desk, and fortunately he looks too hung-over from the weekend to notice me sliding in behind my desk.

"Pass your papers to the front," he's saying, and I feel my stomach do a triple axel as I just now remember the assignment that Gatsby reminded me about yesterday, the five-page critical analysis that we were supposed to do on Hawthorne's "Young Goodman Brown." Throwing a desperate glance straight back over my shoulder, I see my classmates already passing forward their papers. In the midst of it all, Gatsby gives me a quick once-over, and I'm guessing she already knows from my reaction what the problem is. As awkward as it may be, now is probably the time to go up and hit Mr. Bodkins with whatever sob story I can come up with and plead for mercy. I'm just hoping he won't try to stick my tie into the shredder.

The girl behind me hands up a stack of papers and I start to stand, figuring I'll carry them up to Mr. Bodkins along with a story about my dead grandmother. On my feet, I glimpse down at the paper on the top of the pile.

GRAVEN IMAGES:
STARING DOWN THE DEVIL IN HAWTHORNE'S
"YOUNG GOODMAN BROWN"
by Will Shea

I flip through five pages of perfectly cogent literary analysis, typewritten and double-spaced with my name on it, then glance back at Gatsby, stunned. She's not even looking at me.

"Thank you, Mr. Shea." Mr. Bodkins walks by and takes the stack of papers from my hand, and when I look around at

Gatsby again, she's writing something down in her notebook, still not looking at me.

"You didn't have to do that, you know," I tell her later.

We're sitting in the dining hall over lunch — shrimp quesadilla for me, garden salad for her, along with some kind of veggie burger that actually smells amazing considering there's no meat in it. Through the giant wall-size windows, the last swarms of orange leaves are chasing one another in late-October dust devils. The weather's already changing, tilting into winter.

"What makes you think it was me?" she asks.

"The fact that you know what I'm talking about even though I haven't said it yet. Anyway, it really wasn't necessary."

"Right," Gatsby says, taking a big bite of her salad. "Because you had it all worked out."

"Well, I didn't say *that* . . ."

"You didn't have to."

"Thanks for the vote of confidence." I take a bite of my quesadilla, which is crunchy yet tender and bursting with fresh cilantro, and realize that she's still looking at me. "So why did you do it?"

"What?"

"Write that paper for me."

She ponders the question, or pretends to. "Maybe I figured you could use a break after 'falling down the stairs' and busting up your face," Gatsby says, using air quotes for the little white lie I had tried to pass over her in the library yesterday.

"I'm not joking," I say. "You could get suspended for this,

or worse. Why would you take a risk like that for somebody you hardly know?"

She looks at me for a long moment and then sits back, crossing her arms. "I wanted to help you. Is that so hard to swallow?"

"I mean, it's just—you're smart, you're funny, you're pretty." My face is starting to get hot. "Okay, so you work in a library and spend your free time breaking into the rare books when you're depressed, but still . . ."

Now Gatsby's laughing. "You're welcome, okay?" she says, and there's another long silence, one that makes me think maybe I shouldn't have said anything in the first place. "Will?"

"Yeah?"

"What's your secret?"

"What?"

"You know mine. What's yours?"

That stops me, and I just look at her. Suddenly the whole dining hall feels like it's gone silent, and my heart is beating very fast, but Gatsby's merely looking at me with an expression of intelligent curiosity. "What are you talking about?"

"There's something you're not telling anybody, including me."

I force a smile. "What, you're psychic now too?"

"It's just intuition. I noticed it the first time we talked, and it just keeps getting stronger." She blinks. "Tell me, what was it like growing up with missionary parents on the other side of the world?"

For a second there's just more silence between us.

"It was lonely," I say, and a second later, I realize how corny that sounds. But Gatsby doesn't laugh. She doesn't even crack a smile. She just stares back at me.

"Did you have friends there?" she asks. "On your island?"

"Not really."

"Do you miss it?"

"Let's just say I'm a lot happier here."

"I'm glad."

"And I do appreciate your writing the paper."

"It wasn't that big of a deal," she says. "I like Hawthorne."

"Why?"

"He's cool."

"Said nobody ever, in the history of the human race."

"You know, the library has a collection of his original letters and manuscripts."

"Are you sure they're real and not forgeries?" I ask. "Like, not written on My Little Pony stationery or something?"

"Stop it." Gatsby laughs and punches me, hard enough to hurt. "Look," she says, "if it wasn't for me, your precious scholarship would already be in jeopardy, so can we agree to move on?" She waits. I'm just looking at her, a little dazed from either her fist or her generosity. "Seriously, though, what *was* it like?"

"What?"

"Ebeye. Growing up there. I can't imagine. I've never met anyone who's lived in a place like that. Did your parents always know that's what they wanted to do?"

I take in a breath to deliver my spiel but I feel my throat swelling up, like I'm having some kind of allergic reaction to my own lie. Gatsby mistakes my silence for reluctance, as if she's overstepped her bounds, and draws back.

"I get it," she says. "You don't want to talk."

"No," I say, "it's just that—"

"—he doesn't know where to start," a voice says to my right, where Andrea has materialized with her lunch and a stack of books. "Right, Will? That's what happens when you're raised by missionaries. All that humility starts backing up in your system until it floods your brain."

Gatsby turns and regards her coolly. "Hey, Andrea."

"Hello, Gatsby." Andrea sips her coffee. "Happy Monday."

"Thanks," Gatsby says, and she's already getting up, gathering her tray. "I'll see you later, Will?"

"Definitely," I say, as Andrea settles down next to me, emanating a kind of smugness that doesn't even require visual confirmation.

"Well," she says. "*That* looked cozy. Sorry to interrupt."

I roll my eyes. "Please."

"A word of advice, Will. Don't get too close to her. I wouldn't want you to start believing your own lies—especially since you've already tipped your hand to Brandt. Secrets don't last long here."

"Noted." I regard her unemotionally. "Did you want something?"

"As a matter of fact . . ." Andrea opens her backpack and pulls out a leather-bound planner. "I just wanted to go over our little event calendar together." She opens the book to November, where the box representing the twenty-second is circled in red pen. "Now, as you recall, our arrangement ends the week before Thanksgiving break. Today is October 28, which means we've got almost four weeks to get Brandt to hand over fifty thousand. You still want to go through with this?"

"Why?" I say. "You want out? Is being Brandt's pet floozy not paying off like you hoped?"

"Oh my." She smiles. "You really have no clue what you're doing, do you?"

"Watch me," I say.

"Believe me," Andrea says, "I am. So far I've seen you get beat up and thrown out of Casino Night for cheating. Is that your full repertoire, or did you learn any other tricks down in New Jersey?"

"You have no idea."

"You're a hoot, Will." To my surprise, when she smiles again, the delight on her face looks genuine. "No matter how this all comes out, you've already made my year *so* much more interesting. Thank you for that."

"So glad I could be here to amuse you."

"Oh, you do."

And it isn't until Andrea leans over to peck my cheek that I realize Gatsby hasn't left the dining hall yet—she's still standing by the door, watching us. Then she turns and walks away.

SIXTEEN

THE NEXT MORNING I'VE GOT MY ALARM SET EARLY SO I can make it to class without running, but something totally unexpected happens—it snows.

Climbing out of bed, I draw back my curtains to discover a lunar landscape, the campus already covered by a thin but steadily growing layer of white. Thick flurries come whipping down through the branches as the wind blusters along the walkways. *This is crazy,* I think. Down in New Jersey it almost never snows before Thanksgiving.

"Classic early nor'easter," Epic Phil is telling everybody when I get to the dining hall, delivering this news with such authority that you almost expect to see a satellite map behind him. "Freak system must've blown in off the ocean overnight. We haven't even played the Homecoming lacrosse game yet."

There's an excited buzz among the students here, a sense of building anticipation that I don't quite understand. People are filling thermoses with coffee and hot chocolate and carrying their trays out of the cafeteria with them.

"So you think this qualifies?" somebody asks.

"Are you kidding?" Phil says. "This *definitely* qualifies."

"Qualifies for what?" I ask.

He's about to answer me when the entire dining hall falls silent. Dr. Melville walks in, moving to the front of the room with a stiff-legged sense of purpose. I've already been here long enough to know that he doesn't often appear in the dining hall among the students. Right away, I start wondering if this might have something to do with Gatsby and me sneaking into the rare books room over the weekend. What if somebody saw us coming out? I look around the room to see if other authority figures are here, but I don't spot any. Off in the corner, Andrea is cuddled up on Brandt's lap, the two of them watching the proceedings with sleepy-eyed amusement. If Gatsby's here, I don't see her.

Dr. Melville ascends to the lectern at the front of the dining hall and holds up his hands, which doesn't seem to be necessary since the whole room is still noiseless. "Some weather we're having," he says. This statement brings a mystifying burst of cheers and applause. Everybody's watching the head of the school now, and Phil leans over to me and whispers, "If he puts his hat on, it means classes are canceled for the day."

"Why?"

"First snowfall of the year is always Tray Day."

"What's Tray Day?"

"Now, I'd heard we were supposed to get some early flurries . . ." Dr. Melville is saying, and the crowd goes quiet again. "But I was still quite surprised when I went out this morning with my yardstick"—he holds it up and everybody draws in a breath—"and it looks like I'll need to wear this."

He reaches down beneath the podium and pulls out a big

fur-lined, Mad Bomber–style hat, then places it on his head. The entire dining hall explodes with laughter and more cheers. People jump out of their seats, hooting and whistling, and a chant starts going up from the back of the dining hall: "Tray Day, Tray Day, Tray Day . . ."

"What's Tray Day?" I shout at Phil.

"Head out to Monument Hill," he shouts back. "You'll find out."

Monument Hill occupies the northernmost part of campus, an alpine slope covered in white, and by the time I get out there, half the school is already here. Even the faculty has joined in —I see Mr. Bodkins and Dr. Melville and my French instructor, Mademoiselle Lafitte, standing off to the side in ski parkas and mittens, sipping from steaming thermoses and watching the snowball fights, near collisions, and wipeouts. Collie Morgenstern is here snapping pictures for the school's newspaper, *The Connaughton Call*. The snow is more than sufficient for sledding, and I'm at the top of the hill when my phone vibrates in my pocket. It's a text from Uncle Roy, and I can practically hear him growling the words:

> *Flight east canceled due to blizzard in Boston.*
> *Arriving tomorrow, weather permitting. When are*
> *you moving back to civilization, kid??*

"Hey, Will." I look up and see Andrea walking over with her lunch tray. She drops it, takes a seat, and pats the open spot in front of her. "Want to ride down with me?"

"A little snug for two, isn't it?"

"Not if we sit close."

"I'll pass."

She sticks out her tongue, catches a snowflake on it, and licks her lips. "You know, Will," she says, "just because we're competing with each other doesn't mean we can't have a little fun along the way."

"Yeah, well, I'm heading back to the dorm. I'm way behind in U.S. Diplomacy, and—"

"Blah blah blah," she says. "Come on, tough guy. Go big or go home." She nods at my tray, which is still tucked under my arm. "I'll race you. First one to the bottom wins. Unless you're scared."

I look down the hill. It's a long way to the bottom, and the incline is so steep that half the kids are wiping out before they make it to the halfway point.

I'm still deciding when I hear a scream—not a scream of excitement, but one of pain, followed by an eruption of laughter. When I look toward the sound, I see Brandt literally standing on top of a younger kid, most likely a freshman. The kid is face-down and Brandt is jumping on his back with his snowboard, pounding him into the snow. Brandt's pals are gathered around, yukking it up. Everybody else is just standing there with the blank-eyed gaze of bystanders at a car crash.

I act without thinking.

The snowball is in my hand before I even realize I've scooped it up. After packing it tight, I cock my arm and throw it as hard as I can. Usually my aim isn't great, but for some reason this particular throw is perfect, and it drills Brandt so hard in the back of the skull that it knocks him over.

I grab my tray and take a flying leap down the hill.

The lunch tray doesn't handle at all like an actual sled, so I can't steer, and I'm already going way too fast, careening down among kids climbing up the hillside. The sound of snow is hissing in my ear, and wet, cold flakes are flying into my nose and sticking to my eyelashes. Somebody's built a ramp, and I go shooting off into space, airborne for long enough that I hear a voice shout, *"Whoa!"* Then I come crashing back down to earth with a rib-shattering slam, landing at the bottom of the hill in a pile of tangled arms and legs.

A flash goes off in my face as somebody takes my picture, and then the pain follows, gallons of it, trickling in slowly at first, and then faster. I groan and lift my head in time to see a crowd gathered around me. People are laughing. A gloved hand reaches down and yanks me to my feet.

"Careful, Shea," somebody's voice says, slap-brushing snow from my face. "Wouldn't want anything bad to happen to you, now, would you?"

"I think I broke my leg," I mutter.

"Walk it off," the voice says, chuckling. "You'll be fine."

I'm not so sure, but I start limping up the hill anyway. I pass Andrea, standing off to the side with a couple girls I don't recognize. She gives me a wave.

"Looks like you beat me, Shea." She smiles. "Too bad we didn't decide on the stakes, huh?"

"Too bad," I say, nodding.

And I keep walking.

By dinnertime, the flurries have turned to splattery rain, washing away whatever snow had accumulated. I'm on my way out of the dining hall when a kid I've never seen before comes up to me with the school paper.

"Hot off the press," he says, slapping it across my chest and walking away without breaking stride. I look down at the front page.

"King of Tray Day," the headline reads, above a picture of me lying spread-eagle in the snow, my limbs bent and twisted in several unlikely directions.

Then I realize there's something handwritten underneath the photo, two words in all capitals.

CHAPEL. MIDNIGHT.

And underneath it, a single stylized letter *S*.

SEVENTEEN

WHEN I SLIP OUT OF MY DORM AND ARRIVE AT THE chapel at midnight, there's nobody there. I stand outside the main entrance with my hands in my pockets, holding my breath and listening to the sound of melted ice dripping off the pine boughs in the dark, already feeling vaguely foolish. I have no idea what to expect, or how long I'm going to be kept waiting here, or if this is all just an elaborate practical joke at my expense. With every passing minute, the last option seems more and more likely.

I'm getting ready to head back to my room when a voice says, "Wait."

Two figures step out in front of me, both wearing ski masks. I hear a crunch of boots on snow, and when I turn around, three more people are standing there. A half-dozen more appear out of the shadows, and I realize I'm surrounded.

"What's this about?" I ask.

"Follow me." Without another word, one of the masked figures turns and starts making his way toward the cathedral, with the others shadowing him. I get in line to trail the pack. We walk past the arched wooden doors, heading around toward the back, where it's so dark that I can barely see the person walking in front of me. Somebody up ahead flicks a flashlight onto the stone wall, revealing a smaller wooden door with an iron ringbolt on it. The leader takes out a key and unlocks the door, then sets it swinging open. I can see a flight of steps leading underneath the building, and the group makes its way down, single file, into a large bare room.

It's dank down here and even colder than it is outside, and it smells ancient and subterranean, like wet limestone and moss. The noise of our footsteps echoes in the empty space. Vaguely I can make out engravings on the walls around me, crests or insignias, images and writing lost to the gloom. The group has formed a silent circle around me. Their shadows dance and stretch across the walls.

"William Shea," the masked figure in front of me asks, "do you know why you have been brought here?"

"Um," I say, "is it because I'm the king of Tray Day?"

Nobody says anything for a moment. I listen as something sprays against the stone floor, and I catch a whiff of lighter fluid and hear the scrape of a match. All at once the room bursts into flame, a huge letter *S* blazing on the floor in front of me, casting an orange light across the circle of dark-clad figures standing around it. I take a step back.

"The Order of the Sigils has existed here at Connaughton for almost one hundred and fifty years," the voice says. "Our membership is absolutely secret. Every year we invite at least one new student from each class into our ranks. If you choose to accept our invitation, you'll be given an assignment. If you're successful, you'll be inducted into a society as old as the school itself. Your entire life will change, both at Connaughton and afterward. From your induction on, wherever you are, you'll be a Sigil first and everything else second."

I stare at the flames. "What's my assignment?"

"Someone will be in contact with you soon," the voice says, and just like that, somebody turns on a fire extinguisher and the flames gutter out, leaving me in total darkness. There's a faint scuffle of footsteps, then absolute silence.

I stand there for a moment, until my eyes adjust, and then slowly grope my way back up the steps and out into the night.

EIGHTEEN

UNCLE ROY ARRIVES ON THURSDAY, WHICH IS TECHNI-cally Halloween, but I'm too busy to mark the holiday. By then the temperature's shot up twenty degrees, the snow is almost completely melted away, and just like that, it's fall again. People are already wearing light jackets and making jokes about our twenty-four-hour winter. I've never seen a blizzard come and go so fast.

Meanwhile, I'd been thinking about the Sigils, asking around as unobtrusively as possible, trying to figure out what to do. From what little I can learn, invitations to join seem almost random. I've been told that they choose new inductees without regard to how rich their families are, or whether their ancestors came over on the *Mayflower,* or if they are one generation out of the trailer park.

Which makes sense, I guess, considering that they invited me.

At five o'clock that evening I'm walking back from a long study session in the dining hall when a gleaming gray Cadillac pulls up alongside me. For a second the car just sits there, as subtle as a flying saucer, and then the driver's-side window powers down to reveal Roy's deeply tan, wrinkled face behind a pair of enormous mirrored sunglasses. Teeth as white as Tic Tacs gleam out at me in a wide, perfectly even smile.

"Jump in, kid." He doesn't even get out of the car, so I go around to the passenger side with *U.S. Diplomacy Between the World Wars* tucked under my arm. The leather interior smells like a familiar combination of spearmint gum, Brylcreem, and Camel Lights.

"I missed you, Uncle Roy."

Roy reaches over to punch me in the arm. "Good to see you too, William." He's wearing a freshly pressed dark blue Italian suit and a red tie, knotted in a perfect Windsor. He lowers his sunglasses to look at the textbook in my arms. "Studying hard?"

"I've got an exam tomorrow," I say. "I'd like to pass."

"Sure you would." He nods and swings the Caddy around with an authoritative sweep of the arm. "You got a sweet gig going here. Gotta make it look legit, am I right? Sell it to the citizens?"

"Absolutely," I say, and glance down almost guiltily at the history pages that I've been highlighting for the past two hours. The fact is, I started out making crib notes that I could smuggle into class in the palm of my hand and surprised myself by actually reading through the assigned texts and getting lost in the material—in a way that I realize is probably what people mean when they use the word *learning*. I decide to change the subject.

"Nice ride." I nod. "I wasn't aware they still made cars this big."

"You bet," Roy says, consulting the rearview mirror as he plucks at his tie, straightening the knot in some imperceptible way. "I told 'em at Avis that I wasn't about to go driving around in some tuna can. They still got some actual Detroit muscle on the lot. You just gotta ask, is all." As we drive out through the main gates, he whistles. "Beautiful setup here. A little cold for my taste, but classy."

"Uh-huh." There's a second of silence. I glance at him. It's time to talk about why he's really here. "Did you get a chance to check out an office space?"

"North of Boston, a town called Lowell." He accelerates, and the car surges smoothly forward with a low-throated rumble. "Be there in an hour at the most."

We arrive in style forty-five minutes later. The space in question is tucked away in an industrial park outside of downtown, a three-story walkup where all the lights are turned on. There are half a dozen anonymous-looking vehicles scattered around the parking lot and a janitorial van parked in the corner.

"It's perfect," I say.

"You like it?" Roy beams. "I rented out the second floor for a month. Got the office, conference room, reception area— the works. I figure it's more than we need, but it was dirt cheap, and they even threw in a few phone lines. Got the whole thing for three Gs and no questions asked. Come on in and meet the fellas."

"Is everybody here?"

"The whole crew."

I don't ask the next question on my mind, nor do I need to.

As we walk across the parking lot to the stairs, Roy shoots a glance over his shoulder at me.

"I talked to your dad about an hour ago," he says as he climbs the steps, in the same voice that somebody might use to say, *I ran over a rabid skunk on my way to the leper colony.* "Says he's going to meet us here."

Before I can apologize, Roy swings open the second-floor door, ushering me into an empty lobby with faded orange carpeting, all of it just desperate enough to look real for our purposes. I can already hear voices. I follow Roy past a deserted reception desk and into a large, depressing-looking room where six men in their twenties and thirties are standing around, leaning against empty desks, drinking coffee and chatting. There's a pile of computer monitors, phones, and office equipment in the corner and a coffee urn on a table. An open door at the back appears to lead to a smaller, private office. When the men see Uncle Roy and me walk into the room, they all stop talking and look at us.

"Hey, there he is," one of the guys says, holding out his hand for Roy to shake. "Good to see you again, Mr. Devore."

"Likewise." Roy shakes everybody's hand and introduces me around. "William, meet the boys—Rudy Morales, Southie McLaren, Iron Mike Mullen, Lupo Reilly, and the Righteous Brothers." The grin on his face just gets wider. "Fellas, this is my grand-nephew William. He's getting his feet wet on this caper, but he's the brains of the operation. You got any questions about how much cheddar we're gonna squeeze from this chump, you direct them straight to him."

The guys nod and smile. It's pretty obvious they've all worked together before, and they all seem honored just to be sharing a room with a grifter legend like Roy. I know exactly how they feel, and now that they're all staring at me, I get the distinct sensation of being out of my league with men who are all much better at what they do than I am.

"Go ahead, William," Uncle Roy says. "Lay it out."

I draw in a slow breath and tell myself to take it easy. My heart's still pounding hard, but I gradually manage to slow it down.

"Okay," I say. "I don't know how much my uncle's already told you, but here's what it looks like so far." I reach into my *U.S. Diplomacy* textbook and pull out a photo of Brandt. "This is our mark, Brandt Rush—heir to the Rush retail chain. On paper he's worth about sixty million dollars, and that's not counting the shares in his family's Fortune 500 company, which grossed about twenty times that in the last fiscal year alone. We're going to take him only for about two."

"Wait a second." One of the guy's eyebrows shoot up. *"Million?"*

"For starters," I say.

Another guy, one of the Righteous Brothers, lets out a smoky chuckle. "You've got some oysters on you, junior, I'll give you that."

"He gets 'em from his old man," a voice says across the room, and that's when my dad steps in. "How's it going, Billy? Did you tell them it was all my idea?"

Right away it's like all the fun goes out of the room.

Everybody stiffens, and I realize that Roy hasn't told the others about my father being part of this play. Dad doesn't seem to notice, though. He spins a swivel chair around and straddles it, settling in like he owns the place. I can smell the whiskey wafting out of his pores from here. For a second, nobody says anything. Then, from the reception area, I hear a pair of high heels clicking through the doorway, and a woman enters the room and stands behind Dad—the dyed blonde from his motel room.

"Wait a second," Roy says. "Who's *this?*"

"Rhonda's a friend," Dad says breezily, dismissing the question with a wave of the hand. "We need somebody at the front desk, and she's got a secretarial background, don't you, sweetie?"

The guys look at one another, then back at Uncle Roy, who's already got his arms crossed. "No," he says. "No way. No outsiders."

"Come on, Roy," Dad says, leaning back, "you're gonna hurt her feelings."

"I'm gonna hurt a lot more than that," Roy says, "if you don't swivel your girlfriend around and send her back to wherever you found her."

Dad's eyes narrow. "Hey, take it easy."

"Take it easy?" Uncle Roy can't seem to believe his ears. "Let's get something straight, Frank. I didn't even want *you* on this thing, okay? Carting your playmate in here just queered the whole deal."

"Well, that's a shame," Dad says, "because she's *already* in it. See, anything that I didn't get a chance to tell her yet? She just heard the whole scheme through the open door. So . . ." His lips wrinkle back in a yellow, reptilian grin. "I guess we've got nothing left to talk about, huh?"

Uncle Roy's nostrils flare wide open and I can see the war going on beneath the muscles of his face. He doesn't want to walk out on this deal, but everything inside him—every instinct of self-preservation that's kept him out of jail through-out his adult life—is screaming that this isn't safe. Finally, he just shakes his head like a fighter shaking off a punch.

"You better vouch for her," he mutters under his breath.

"Sure," Dad says flippantly, and settles back as though the outcome was never in doubt. He turns to the other guys in the room, all of whom suddenly look as though they wish they were somewhere else. "You boys all know the online poker racket, or you need me to run it down with you?"

Uncle Roy shakes his head. "William's gonna tell it."

"Of course," Dad says, and smiles. "I wouldn't have it any other way."

"It works like this," I say. "I'm going to bring Brandt here and introduce him to the office. He's going to sit down to play, and halfway through the hand, he's going to get a text on his cell phone from one of you guys, telling him how to bet. The bet pays off, of course, and he doubles his money, so he wants to go again. In fact, because he's already got it in for my fake boss—Brian McDonald—he'll want to go big enough so that when he wins, he'll put the whole operation out of business. I'm figuring two million."

"Wait a second. One thing I don't get." One of the guys —Lupo Reilly, I think—shakes his head when I finish talking. "What teenage kid can actually get his hands on two million bucks?"

"I've personally seen it happen," I tell him. "Since his dad's accountants let him manage his own portfolio, Brandt has got an almost unlimited trust fund that he can draw from. They let him play the market. They say it's good practice for when he takes over the family fortune. And best of all"—I take a deep breath—"Brandt already thinks that this McDonald guy is trying to get revenge on him for what Brandt did to his daughter Moira. So now it's personal."

"You're sure about that part?" Uncle Roy asks.

"Trust me," I say. "He's vindictive as hell." I turn to face the group. "Tomorrow night I'll bring Brandt down here to check out the operation. He'll see how it all works. Dad will play Mr. McDonald, acting like he's still bitter about what Brandt did to Moira, but when Brandt puts down the cash I'm fronting him for the first bet, McDonald will start to change his tune and suck up to him. Hopefully it'll just make Brandt want to scam him for even more."

"I like it," Dad says, and shoots a grin at Rhonda, who's been busily chewing her gum. "Of course, I should. Since the whole thing's my idea."

Uncle Roy grimaces. "That's my least favorite part of the whole deal."

"I'll need about two thousand in cash to front Brandt tomorrow," I tell him.

"No problem." Roy opens his wallet and peels off a crisp stack of hundreds, handing them over. "And I'll have the boys here hook you up with some dummy credit cards. They bill to a shell corporation in the Caymans, so once the charges catch up to us in a few weeks, we'll be long gone. Just don't charge anything big. No real estate, nothing like that, you got it?"

"Got it," I say, as Lupo Reilly hands me a Visa and an American Express. "In the meantime, I'll get Brandt buttered up for the deal, let him know how much Mr. McDonald has been talking smack about him."

"Good, kid, but don't oversell it," Uncle Roy says. "We don't want Richie Rich hating us so much that he decides not to come back."

"Believe me, I know this guy," I say. "The angrier he gets, the deeper he'll want to get involved."

"Sounds like my kind of sucker." Uncle Roy looks at me with narrowed eyes. "Is there anything else I need to know at this point?"

Andrea's face flashes through my mind, but I decide now is not the time to bring up our bet. I shake my head. "I don't think so."

"So we'll see you tomorrow."

I nod and turn to go. "I'll be here."

"Hey, William," Uncle Roy says, his hand falling on my shoulder, "you mind if me and the boys stick around for a while and talk through some of the details?"

"No problem," Dad says, and grins at me. "I'll drive him home."

NINETEEN

YOU DIDN'T TELL HIM, DID YOU?" DAD ASKS, OUT IN THE parking lot.

"Tell him what?"

His face pinches. "Don't play me for a patsy, kid. I invented this racket."

For a second we just stand there in the exhaust-reeking, cold darkness outside the office building. Rhonda has already climbed into Dad's old Chevy and now she's sitting in the passenger seat, having swapped out her gum for a Marlboro, fiddling impatiently with the car radio.

"I know why you're in such a hurry to pull off this scam," he says, peering at me from under his eyebrows. "I know all about your Thanksgiving bet."

I stare at him. "What—?"

"Your little friend from school paid me a visit the other day. What's her name—Andrea? She must have seen you leaving my motel in town, because she came by later and told me everything." He tilts his chin up so that I can almost see a ghost of a smile tucked into the corner of his mouth. "Gutsy move on your part, seeing who can fleece this Rush brat first."

I don't say anything.

"Don't worry," Dad says. "Your secret's safe with me. Still,

I gotta say, it's a good thing you didn't go against me on bringing Rhonda into it." He makes a fist and chucks me on the
chin, hard enough to hurt. "I'd hate to break up our father-son
bond, right?"

"Just make sure you're here tomorrow," I say.

"Oh, I'll be here," Dad says. "For two million bucks, I
wouldn't miss it for the world."

We drive back in silence.

When I get to my dorm room, my weekend assignments are
piling up on my desk—course packs, textbooks, unfinished
papers, two chapters for Global Risk, and about a hundred
pages of U.S. Diplomacy, plus math and English Lit—but I can't
concentrate on any of it. I can't stop thinking about what Dad
told me about Andrea, how she went to him with everything.
Of course it makes sense that she'll do whatever she has to do
to derail the con, and I know it means I just have to step up my
game, but something in me is resisting.

I force myself to open a textbook and start reading about
Wilson's Fourteen Points, but almost instantly there's a tap-
ping on my window.

I go over and push the curtains aside. Gatsby's standing
out there with her arms crossed, looking in at me. Her hair is
tucked up into a black knit cap and her breath is steaming out
in clouds. She looks cold. I flip the latch and swing the window
open.

"Hey." Her cheeks are flushed, and she tosses a quick look
over her shoulder. "Can I come in?"

"Sure," I say. "What's up?"

"It's complicated." She climbs through the window, ducking her head down, and I notice that she's wearing a huge black nylon backpack. Whatever's inside is bulky enough that it almost catches on the window frame. Once she's inside, she shuts the window and yanks the curtains closed behind her, turns around, and looks at me. Her glasses are starting to steam up and she takes them off to rub the lenses on her scarf. "So," she says, sounding out of breath and sitting down on my bed. "How are you?" She takes off her gloves and gives me a weak smile.

"Uh, fine," I say. "What's—"

There's a sudden banging on my door. Gatsby shoots up like she's on springs, her head swiveling in all directions, looking around the room. The knocking continues, becoming more insistent.

"Who is it?" I say.

"Security. I'm looking for Ms. Haverford," a man's voice says. It's familiar, but I'm not sure why. "I know she's in there. Open the door, Mr. Shea."

I look at Gatsby, but she's frantically struggling with the backpack, taking it off and shoving it under my bed, where it barely fits.

"You've got the wrong room," I say. "This is an all-male floor."

There's silence for a second, and then I hear keys rattling outside the door. Apparently the guard has had enough with the small talk and is already letting himself in.

"Okay, all right," I say. "Just hold on." I'm trying to stall, but the door's opening. From the corner of my eye I see Gatsby crawling under the bed next to her backpack.

Seconds later, a uniformed man steps inside. It's George from the other night, the Kant-reading security guard who let me into Brandt's dorm. His face and neck are flushed like he's been running, and he smells faintly of tobacco.

"Where is she?" he asks, craning his neck to look around the room.

"Who?"

"Don't play stupid with me, Shea."

"Look," I say, "I told you, I'm alone here. And as you can see"—I point at my desk and the mountain of papers and books —"I've got a ton of studying to do. So if you don't mind . . ."

"Nice," George says, lifting one of Gatsby's gloves off my bed and holding it up for closer examination. "Not really your color, though, is it?"

"I found 'em outside. Going to put them in lost and found in the morning."

"Uh-huh." After crossing the room, he opens my closet and starts yanking out my clothes. Once he's finished trashing my wardrobe, George takes another walk around the room and ends up next to the window, staring out at the night. Then he looks at me.

"I told you," I say.

George's whole face clenches, and then he just shakes his head and walks out. The door clicks shut. I wait until I hear his footsteps fade down the wooden hallway. Then I exhale.

"He's gone," I say.

Gatsby comes sliding out from under the bed, brushing herself off. "Wow," she says, "you've got a lot of dust under there."

"Are you going to tell me why security is looking for you?"

"I accidentally tripped an alarm in the rare books collection tonight."

"What? Why?"

She reaches under the bed for the backpack, unzips it all the way, and pulls out the Gutenberg Bible. For a second I just stare at it, this historical artifact lying on my bed next to an empty Mountain Dew bottle and a rumpled T-shirt.

"Okay," I say, "that's the Gutenberg Bible—"

"The *fake* Gutenberg."

"You stole it?"

"Borrowed it."

"Okay, but I'm pretty sure this particular item doesn't circulate."

"Will, listen." She looks up at me, absolutely serious. "We just need you to hold on to it for a while."

"*We?*"

"It's important. Consider it an assignment."

"An *assignment?* Wait, you mean . . ." For a second, it's dead silent, as if all of the air has been sucked out of the room, and Gatsby's face is expressionless. "*You're* in the Sigils?"

"Is that such a shock?"

"Well, kind of, yeah." Then it hits me. "Are you the one who nominated me for membership?"

Gatsby allows herself the slightest smile. "I knew you were smart."

"Why me?"

"For one thing," she says, "you threw that snowball."

"What?"

"At Brandt's head. On Tray Day. Nobody's ever done anything like that before."

"That? It was just a lucky toss. I didn't even think it would hit him." Then the implications of what she's saying finally occur to me. "Wait. You mean, Brandt's not a Sigil?"

"Are you kidding?" Gatsby laughs out loud at the thought of it. "The Sigils are the antidote to the Brandt Rushes of the world. We're outsiders, Will." The laughter has drained away from her face. "Like you."

I just look back at her. For an instant the room is absolutely quiet again. I'm an outsider, all right. She has no idea.

"Now," Gatsby says, and nods at the Gutenberg, "in order to prove yourself worthy of the Sigils, you have to complete this assignment. Keep this in your room for one week. If you can do that without getting caught, you'll be inducted into full membership."

I shake my head. "I don't understand. Why the Gutenberg, other than it's incredibly difficult to hide?"

"Funny you should ask," she says. "It took some digging, but I did some research on the school's acquisition of the Bible. You know how I said it was purchased thirty years ago from a rare-book dealer in the U.K.? The school actually got it for a bargain-basement price, under one condition—that the book dealer's son got a full scholarship here. Any guesses what his name was?"

"I give up."

Gatsby can't hide her smile. "Melville."

"Wait." I blink at her. "As in, the head of the school?"

"That's him."

"Dr. Melville's father sold the fake Gutenberg to the school?" Now I'm smiling back at her. "That's unbelievable. Do you think he knew at the time?"

"Well," Gatsby says, "the fact that Melville senior disappeared not long afterward, never to be heard from again, should tell us something, shouldn't it?" She lowers her voice. "I wonder if maybe Melville himself knew about it too, even then."

The idea that Dr. Melville might have been in on it—a father-and-son con team—hits way too close to home, and all at once I feel myself straining to change the subject. "That thing's huge." I glance down at the enormous Bible again. "How am I supposed to stash it in my room for a week?"

"I don't know," she says. "Hang a picture on it and disguise it as a wall?"

"No, seriously. What if security comes back through here with Bible-sniffing dogs or something?"

"You'll figure it out." She's getting ready to climb out the window and it occurs to me that in a few seconds she'll be gone, that all I'll have is the smell of her shampoo in my room and the emptiness where she was standing. And I realize that, no matter what happens, I need to mark this moment somehow in my mind so that I can come back to it again.

"Hey," I say.

"What?"

I take a deep breath in. "You know how Homecoming is on Friday?"

"It hasn't escaped my attention," she says.

"Are you going?"

"That's tomorrow." She narrows her eyes. "Are you seriously asking me to Homecoming?"

"It starts at seven."

"Will—"

"Just say yes," I tell her. "Before you have time to talk yourself out of it."

Gatsby looks at me for a moment in silence.

"You'll need a tuxedo," she says.

"I'll rent one in town."

"Can you afford that?"

"I'll figure it out." I wait. "So is that a yes?"

She smiles. "Seven o'clock. I'll meet you there," she says.

And that's how she leaves me, with a fake Gutenberg on my bed and the promise of something better, as she climbs back out the window and into the night.

TWENTY

THE NEXT MORNING I'M OFF TO BREAKFAST WITH MY senses on high alert. I don't know what I'm expecting—blaring headlines in the school paper, room-to-room searches, security guards doing random bag checks —but there's no word about the missing Gutenberg Bible. It's like nothing's even happened. Everybody's just going about his or her regular routine. Halfway to the dining hall it occurs to me that if Dr. Melville knows his Bible is a fake, then the last thing he'd want to do is draw attention to its disappearance. Maybe Gatsby's actually done him a favor.

Meanwhile, the Bible itself is safely tucked up under my bed, stuffed inside a hole that I've cut in my box spring and then duct-taped shut. I have no idea how safe it really is there, or how stupid it is that I'm potentially jeopardizing the con by keeping the Bible in my room when I could've easily just refused the assignment. My motives don't make sense, even to me. I'm a city kid from New Jersey. Why do I want to join the Sigils anyway?

We're outsiders, Will. Like you.

The thought gives me chills. I keep thinking about how her hair tickled my neck when we were leaning over the glass case in the rare books collection. The tiny, almost imperceptible smile on her face when I asked her to Homecoming. Standing in line with my tray, I can remember exactly how she smells, the sound of her voice, her chalky little laugh, and I realize that my heart's beating way too hard.

I shut my eyes and open them again slowly.

I can't afford to feel this way about her.

I'm not going to be here that long.

Outside the dining hall, horns are honking and people are calling out to one another with big fake cheerful hellos. Homecoming Weekend at Connaughton is like a combination of summer in the Hamptons and a royal wedding. The campus parking lot is packed with Mercedes and Rolls-Royces, high-end BMWs and the occasional Lamborghini, as parents, alumni, and families arrive. At least two private helicopters have already touched down, and I spot bodyguards with earpieces and mirrored sunglasses hovering outside the dining hall.

Later that morning I get "my" Hawthorne paper back with a big red A written across the top. *Excellent work,* Mr. Bodkins's spiky handwriting enthuses. *Very insightful writing. I look forward to reading more from you.* Standing there with the essay in my hands, I feel a throb of guilt go through my chest followed by the sudden, self-destructive urge to go to him and confess that I didn't write a word of it.

That afternoon I take the bus to town to rent a tuxedo. There's a florist on Main Street, where I pick out a corsage and a dozen long-stemmed red roses. On the way back to the bus stop, I walk past an antique shop on the corner, and something in the window grabs my attention. Looking more closely I see that it's an early printing of the first volume of Hawthorne's *Twice-Told Tales*.

I go inside and ask the woman behind the counter about the book.

"You've got excellent taste," she says, lifting it from the window display and handing it to me. "That's a rare edition."

"How much?"

"Three hundred."

"Will you take a credit card?"

I hold my breath while she swipes the AmEx that Lupo Reilly gave me, but the authorization goes through without a problem. After signing the sales slip, I slide the book under my coat and head out the door. It's getting colder, but I don't even feel it.

By the time I get to the bus stop, I'm whistling.

Back at Connaughton, I realize that I don't have any wrapping paper. My eyes settle on my tattered old map of the Pacific, the one with Ebeye on it. I wrap the map around the Hawthorne book and it fits perfectly. I don't even have to trim the edges.

I grab an early dinner, take an extra-long scalding hot shower, and begin to get ready for the night. The tux looks great but my hair's all wrong. It's already too long, and it sticks out to the side like a crow's broken wing in a way that no amount of gel is going to make better. In the end I just abandon it, gather up the flowers and Hawthorne book, and step outside.

The night is clear and cold, and the grounds are strung with lights for the evening. Far off in the distance, I can hear music and laughter coming from the Manse, which, for all intents and purposes, is the center of the universe tonight.

Besides being the single oldest building on campus, the Manse is also the home for all of Connaughton's formal dances and assemblies, a combination of nineteenth-century ballroom and private castle. According to tradition, it's the place where families gather before the Homecoming game each year, a chance for millionaire alumni to compare notes while their ungrateful kids ignore them entirely. It's a little weird that parents are invited to the dance, but it also makes sense in a creepy, ultrarich, incestuous kind of way that probably dates back to Medieval Europe. As I step inside, I see designer dresses, hear the laughter and chatter floating out.

Gatsby's nowhere to be seen.

"Hey, Will."

Looking around, I see Andrea standing close by, smiling at me. For a second I almost don't even recognize her. Her hair is pinned up in shimmering braids to expose her long slender throat, and she is wearing what might be charitably described as a black spider web connected by silver rings. It's made out of some kind of expensive shimmery material that I think is officially known as "trying way too hard." Still, she looks great, and she knows it. Even Brandt seems to be paying attention.

"Nice tux." She reaches out to touch my lapel, then looks

down at the roses and the book that I'm holding. "Where's your date?"

"She's on her way."

"Of course she is," Andrea says, turning. "By the way, have you met Brandt's parents?"

I look behind her at the two people standing there in formalwear, and right away I feel the difference between them and everyone else in the room.

There's rich, and then there's *rich*—and then there's Herbert and Victoria Rush.

The most disturbing thing about extremely wealthy white people is how they all look vaguely related, as if they were grown in the same lab, somewhere in the Connecticut suburbs.

For a moment the Rushes don't speak, at least not to me. Standing there side by side like a pair of binary stars, they seem to exude their own private atmosphere, a weirdly selective gravitational field that sucks in the lucky few while flinging all the rest of us indiscriminately into the dreary void of middle-class hopelessness. Even this close, I get the strange feeling that they aren't seeing me at all. I can't help but wonder what I must look like through Rush vision—am I just some Vaseline-smeared blur, a black-and-white pixelation, like the faces of passersby whose identities are protected on reality TV? Or do I look like some visual annoyance, like one of those floaty things that just hover in the corner of your eye and won't go away?

Either way, I'm clearly not part of their world.

"Mr. and Mrs. Rush," Andrea says, "this is Will Shea. Will's here from a tiny little island in the South Pacific. His parents were missionaries, right, Will?"

"Oh?" Victoria Rush gives me a tight smile. "How interesting." After an appropriate amount of silence, she goes back to ignoring me. "My goodness, isn't *anyone* going to dance?"

As if on cue, the music starts playing, some old song from the '50s, and I watch as Brandt leads Andrea to the center of the dance floor. It's pageantry, pure and simple — slow and easy and elegant. Brandt lifts Andrea's arm and whirls her around, the look on his face never changing from the blank, phoned-in expression of a rich kid doing a job, playing a role, knowing that it's all part of inheriting a fortune so great that even he can't count it all. In the middle of everything, Andrea catches my eye and winks. I keep looking around for Gatsby, wondering where she is, if she's coming, if something happened, as the weight in my stomach gets heavier and heavier.

When the song ends, Andrea makes her way to the punch bowl and then back over to me. "Well, that was fun." She lifts her gaze to meet mine, and she looks again at the roses that I'm still carrying around, along with the gift-wrapped book and the corsage. "Still alone?" She checks her watch. "It's getting late, isn't it?"

"Thanks for your concern."

"Poor Will." She touches my arm. "Rejection doesn't suit you."

I turn and walk through the ballroom again, but I still can't find Gatsby anywhere. I check my phone. No messages. When

I call her, it goes straight to voice mail. After the beep, I start talking.

"Hey, Gatsby, it's Will. I'm here at the dance. Just making sure everything's—"

A fist thumps me on the shoulder. It's Brandt, right behind me. "Yo, Willpower. We still on for tonight?"

Clicking off the phone, I turn around and look him in the eye.

"Sure."

"Good." He looks more alive now than he has all night. "Meet me out front by the statue in twenty minutes. Don't be late."

After he walks away, I make one more circle through the room, but now I know she's not coming, and I can feel people starting to stare at me, hear them talking behind my back. I leave the dance and make my way across the almost empty campus to Gatsby's dorm. There's a light in her third-floor window. For a moment I just stand there, holding the roses and the corsage and the book, watching a shadow move across her curtains.

I call again.

Voice mail.

I stuff the book back under my coat. The roses and corsage go into the trash outside her dorm, and I head out to find Brandt.

I've got work to do.

TWENTY-ONE

THE PLAN IS SIMPLE. I'M SUPPOSED TO MEET BRANDT IN front of the statue of Lancelot Connaughton, where Uncle Roy will pick us up and drive us down to Lowell. With any luck, tonight's trial run will pay off. By next week, Brandt will want to double his money, then go for the big payout with plenty of time before our deadline.

Like I said. Simple.

Except . . .

I can't stop thinking about Gatsby. Right now I've got two thousand dollars of Uncle Roy's cash in my back pocket, and the entire success or failure of the con depends on how I play things tonight. But my thoughts keep circling back to Gatsby. What she was thinking. Why she didn't call. Why she stood me up.

This is obviously not the frame of mind that I need to be in right now.

I stand outside in my tuxedo, watching the breath steam out of my mouth in clouds, looking at the puritanical face of Lancelot Connaughton. If he has any insight into my situation, he's not sharing it.

A hand lands on my shoulder.

"Yo, bro, you ready to rock?"

I turn around. Brandt is standing there with Carl beside him, silent and stoic. Like Brandt and me, Carl is still wearing a tux. Unlike Brandt and hopefully me, he still looks like a caveman on Oscar night. "Hey." I look Carl up and down. "You forgot your lacrosse stick."

"He doesn't need it," Brandt says.

"You were supposed to come alone."

"Change of plans," Brandt says. "That's not a problem, is it, Will?"

I shake my head. The last-minute switch gets my adrenaline going and puts my head back in the game. I'm actually glad for it.

"Good," Brandt says. "You bring the filthy lucre?"

I reach into my pocket and take out the roll, twenty one-hundred-dollar bills. "When we get to Mr. McDonald's office, he's going to show you the different online poker games and ask you how much you want to bet. Start small and let him convince you to go the full two grand."

Brandt looks scornfully at the cash. "Thanks, but I think I can handle myself."

"Just be careful with this," I say, handing over the money. "It's all I could get my hands on for now."

"Just tell me how I'm gonna win."

"My partner will be texting you messages throughout the hand," I say, "telling you how much to bet. Just do exactly what the messages say. You'll win."

"You must be pretty sure of your system."

"It's foolproof."

"It better be."

That's as far as he gets as a pair of headlights come streaming up the long drive heading toward the statue. At first I think it's Uncle Roy, and then I realize I'm wrong. The lights belong to one of the campus-security vehicles taking a slow cruise around the service road, and it pulls up in front of us, stopping on the other side of the statue. I hear the door open, and I see George the Kant-reading security guard step out.

Brandt glances up at him breezily. "Hey, Georgie-boy. Nice night, huh?"

The guard walks over to us. "What are you doing out here? Why aren't you at the dance?"

Nobody says anything, and I realize he's talking to Carl— which isn't a huge surprise when I suddenly realize how much the two of them look alike. George is basically an older version of Carl. The resemblance is uncanny.

"He's hanging out with me, George," Brandt says. "Thought I'd do him a favor."

George doesn't say anything.

"I mean, hey," Brandt says, "maybe he'd be better off at public school. Finishing his senior year with a bunch of middlebrow losers. What do you think?"

George keeps quiet and just looks at Carl, who glares back at his father, nothing but eighteen inches of flash-frozen silence suspended between them. Face-to-face, their chiseled profiles look like one of those optical illusions where you start to see the outline of some mysterious third shape appearing between them.

"Are you going somewhere?" George asks.

Carl squares his shoulders. "Why do you care?"

"It's a closed campus. There are rules."

"Like *you've* ever cared about them," Carl says, in a voice that's half snarl, half whisper.

"Listen, son . . ." George draws in a breath. He looks like he wants to say something but has no idea where to begin.

"Better move along, George," Brandt says. "Wouldn't want to be late on your nightly routine. A guy in your position can't afford too many more strikes against him, am I right?"

George sighs but gets back into his truck and drives away, leaving the three of us alone in the moonlight.

"Your guy is late," Brandt says.

Before I can answer, I see a pair of headlights coming toward us.

"Here he is now," I say.

TWENTY-TWO

WHEN UNCLE ROY'S CADILLAC PULLS UP, I OPEN THE back door and slide inside. Roy's behind the wheel, but he doesn't turn around or say anything until Carl starts to climb in next to Brandt.

"Hold on," Roy growls, looking back over his shoulder. "Who's the gorilla?"

"Carl's with me," Brandt says.

Roy shakes his head. "No deal." He points to me with an index finger the size of a gun barrel. "Mr. McDonald said just your friend. Nobody else." He turns to Carl. "Take a hike, Gargantua."

Nobody says anything for a second, and Brandt shrugs. "Fine, whatever." He points at Carl, still halfway on the sidewalk, like he's a pet dog. "Stay."

Carl takes a step back, leaving me and Brandt in the back seat while Uncle Roy guns it through the main gates and back down the country road that leads us to the highway, heading south. There's not a lot of small talk. Brandt stretches his legs and gets out his phone, checking his messages, looking at something on Twitter, sending a few texts. He seems totally relaxed and in charge of the situation. Without glancing up from his phone, he says, "So the library freak stood you up, huh?"

I swallow hard. "We're just friends."

"Dude, that's pathetic."

"What?"

"I can't decide what's worse, you crushing on some troll who paints her nails with black Sharpie, or the fact that you couldn't even get her to show up at the dance." Brandt turns to me, apparently serious. "You can't let yourself get humiliated like this. You're supposed to be a player." He pronounces it "playa" in true white-boy hip-hop fashion. "You know what I mean?"

"Thanks for the advice."

"Trust me, it's for the best," Brandt says, and leans forward to Uncle Roy. "Hey, driver. How much longer is this going to take?"

"We're almost there," Uncle Roy says.

"Next time we're taking my helicopter." Brandt cranes his head forward again. "How long have you been working for this guy McDonald, anyway?"

Uncle Roy doesn't answer.

"You know about his daughter?"

"I know she's a very nice girl," Uncle Roy says. "And if you got anything more to say about it, you can feel free to hop out of this car anytime." His eyes flash in the rearview mirror. "Or I can toss you out on your ear—it's all the same to me."

Brandt smirks but doesn't say anything.

It's silent all the rest of the way to Lowell.

When Uncle Roy stops the car in the lot of the industrial park, Brandt sits in the back like he's waiting for somebody to jump out and open the door for him. When nobody does, he opens it himself, extends one lanky leg, and steps out, then follows Uncle Roy and me toward the rundown office building.

"This is his base of operations?" Brandt shakes his head. "What a dump."

Uncle Roy doesn't say anything as we walk up the steps and into the second-floor lobby. I walk past the reception desk and enter the main workspace. Everything is in place, looking better than I could've hoped.

The guys that Uncle Roy brought up from Boston—Iron Mike, the Righteous Brothers, Lupo Reilly, Southie McLaren, Rudy Morales—are all sitting in front of computer workstations, guzzling energy drinks and talking on their phones. None of them even looks up at us as we walk by. Glancing down, I see lines and columns of code scrolling up the screens. Dad's girlfriend, Rhonda, walks by with a pot of coffee in one hand and a cell phone in the other. In other words, everything looks perfect.

"Where's Mr. McDonald?" Roy asks.

"In his office," she says without breaking stride, and cocks her head at the closed door on the far side of the room before throwing a glance my way. "He's already pissed at you for not showing up earlier."

I frown. "Who, me? I told him where I was going."

Brandt snickers. "Sounds like you've got some brown nosing to do, Will. Good thing you've had a lot of practice."

"Come on," Roy says, waving us to the back of the room. "Let's hope he's in a good mood."

The back office is brightly lit and cleaner than the rest of the property, with a halogen lamp in the corner and fresh paint on the walls. Dad's pacing behind the desk, talking on the phone. Next to an open laptop there's a framed picture of Moira McDonald—a nice touch that I thought of myself.

Dad sees us step in, scowls, and holds up one finger. Brandt gives him an eye roll that is the exclusive province of American entitlement, but he still manages to stand there while Dad finishes talking.

"Yeah, well, you tell him I said we need to shave the extra one-point-one by tomorrow morning, or he's cut off. Those exact words—that's right." He clicks off and jabs a finger at me. "Where the hell were you?"

"Mr. McDonald—" I start.

"Valerie tells me that you've been out of the office all day." Dad turns to Roy. "And nobody says a word to me about it?" Finally he pivots to unleash his glare on Brandt. "Who's this idiot?"

"Mr. McDonald," I say, "meet Brandt Rush."

Dad doesn't say anything. He just stares at Brandt with a glare that could cut diamonds. Brandt looks back at him, then saunters forward a half step and picks up the picture of Moira from on top of the desk, holding it up by two fingers and keeping it at arm's length.

"I've seen better pictures of her," he says, and flicks his eyes up at Dad. "How's your daughter doing, anyway, Mr. McDonald?"

Dad's jaw tightens, and when he speaks, his voice is low and steady. "You want to put that down right now, my friend. Or you're gonna lose that hand."

"Hey, no harm, no foul." Brandt drops the picture onto the desk, where it hits the surface with a clatter. "I'm just a concerned citizen. Wish her well, that's all."

"Moira finished her senior year at Andover," Dad says, through clenched teeth. "She's fine. Graduated with honors."

"Yeah?" Brandt gives a big, theatrical yawn. "That's too bad. Pretty mediocre school compared to Connaughton. Which means she probably fit right in, huh?"

"That's it." Dad turns to Uncle Roy. "Louie, haul this worthless piece of garbage out of my sight. And see that he falls down the stairs a few times on the way."

Roy gestures. "Come on, kid."

"I'm worth half a billion dollars," Brandt says, not budging. He gives Dad a half-lidded smirk. "If anything happens to me, I promise you, you're a dead man."

"I'm all a-tremble," Dad says, and nods to Roy. "You heard me—get him out."

Uncle Roy reaches for Brandt's elbow, and Brandt yanks it away. Roy hauls back like he's about to swing at him, and that's when I step forward to play my part.

"Mr. McDonald," I say, "just hold on. Brandt only wants to place a bet."

"A bet?" Dad says. "I run an online operation, you moron —and you bring him here to the office?"

"He wants to do it in person." I shrug. "He's old school that way, right, Brandt?"

Brandt doesn't say anything, just stands there with his hands in his pockets. For a second the only sound is the noise from the main workspace outside Dad's office.

Finally Dad sits down behind his desk and looks at Brandt without a trace of expression. I can tell that he's sober, which means he's handling this perfectly. I feel an odd thrill of admiration for him, even respect, an unexpected reminder of what he's actually capable of when he's bringing his A-game. His eyes remain on Brandt, and they are the cold, calculating eyes of a man with an operation to protect.

"How big a bet?" he says.

"Two grand," I say. "He just wants to—"

"I'm not talking to you." Dad is still staring at Brandt. "You know what my daughter said to me after you posted those pictures of her on Facebook, you degenerate piece of garbage? She said she wished she had never been born. That's a direct quote. You know what that kind of humiliation feels like?"

"Yeah, well." Brandt grins. "The truth hurts, doesn't it? By the way . . ." He leans in, just a little, and lowers his voice slightly. "I've still got some copies of those pictures if you want 'em. Suitable for framing."

Dad's fingers are gripping the desk so tightly that I can see his knuckles turning white. I can also see the veins in his head now. He's selling this so well that it's a little scary.

"Two grand, Mr. M.," I say. "Cash. It'll be quick. Then we'll be out of here."

Dad closes his eyes and opens them again. His pupils pop to Uncle Roy. "Get him a laptop."

"I thought you said—"

"*Just do it.*" Dad looks back at Brandt, his voice tight. "I'll take your money, kid. Every penny. And the sooner I do it, the sooner I can scour your stench from my office."

Twenty minutes later, we're out of there as promised, Brandt following me into the back seat of the Caddy with an extra two thousand dollars in his pocket.

"Well, what do you think?" I say, just as Uncle Roy gets behind the wheel. "Smooth, right?"

Brandt doesn't say anything as Uncle Roy drives us back to Connaughton. He fidgets with his phone, then sits back and stares out the window. I try to imagine what he's thinking. He just won two grand in three hands of online poker, while "my associate"—really just Lupo Reilly in the main office—texted him how to bet. The system itself wasn't difficult to work out, and since Dad never seemed to notice Brandt checking his iPhone, Brandt must have assumed he got away with it. Which is exactly how we want to leave it.

Uncle Roy drops us off in front of the statue of Lancelot Connaughton. For a second we both just stand there, shivering. Then Brandt looks at me.

"When can we go back?" he asks.

I take my time before answering, making sure I get exactly

the right expression on my face. "We should probably hang back a bit. If we come back too soon, it'll be obvious that—"

"Next Friday. I want to do another test run. Ten thousand this time."

I shake my head. No doubt Uncle Roy has the cash to pay out a ten-thousand-dollar win, but I'm not sure he can get his hands on it that quickly. "You saw it work," I say. "If we go back too many times—"

"One more test run," Brandt says. "If it works, I'll front you the full two mill for the big score. I want to bring him down hard." He glares at me. "You want to get this guy, right, Shea? For slapping your mom around?"

"Yeah, of course, but—"

"Then make it happen."

And he leaves me standing there.

TWENTY-THREE

THE NEXT DAY IS THE HOMECOMING LACROSSE MATCH. Tuesday's freak snowstorm is a distant memory, and the manicured field is green and dry. Even though I don't understand the game, I'm sitting in the stands with a fresh cup of coffee, watching Connaughton trounce the hopeless schmoes from St. Albans, who—even to my uneducated eye—seem to have forgotten which end of the stick to hold on to. The score is already 3–0. Around me the stands are full of parents and alumni dressed in the school colors, drinking their lattes and cheering every play. Six rows down, Brandt and Andrea are side by side, sharing a blanket. I'm not sure what canoodling is, but I'd be willing to bet they're doing it.

"Can I sit here?"

I look up and see Gatsby standing in front of me. She looks tired, her face pale in the morning light, her hands plunged deep in the pockets of her coat.

"Oh," I say. "Hey."

"Listen," she says, "about last night . . ."

"Yeah."

"I'm sorry."

She just stands there. I'm waiting for more, some kind of explanation, but there isn't anything else. "It's cool."

"Thanks."

"Are you all right? I tried to call . . ."

"I'm fine," she says.

"Was it some kind of Sigils thing?" I ask. "Like, another test or something? Because, I mean, if that's what it was . . ."

"No," she says. "It wasn't anything like that."

"Oh. Okay."

There's a silence between us that seems to last forever. It's like there's this soundproof bubble around us, and the rest of the world is sealed away somewhere on the other side of it, going about its business, remote and unreal. Sometimes that kind of privacy can feel good—intimate, special. Not this time.

"I came by your room," I say. "I saw the light on."

"Will." Gatsby lowers her eyes. "That whole thing. It was a mistake."

"Which part?"

"When you invited me to the dance . . ." She looks back up at me. "I shouldn't have said yes."

"Why not? Is it something I did?"

She shakes her head. "You didn't do anything." Somewhere down on the field something happens and the crowd cheers, and we just keep looking at each other.

"Listen," she says, "I'll see you around, okay?"

"Sure," I say, and my voice sounds strange to me, like it's being piped in from some completely different person.

And I watch her go.

• • •

I look down at Brandt and Andrea, snuggling together under the blanket. I couldn't care less what they're doing, but I find myself wondering if Brandt's said anything to her about our trip down to Lowell last night. Then, right on cue, Andrea turns around, looks up at me, and wrinkles her nose.

On the field, it's halftime, and I see Dr. Melville walking across the playing turf with a microphone. Behind him, a pair of students are carrying out some kind of banner, unfurling it along the field. From here I can see that it's a flag, deep blue with white and orange bands and a star in the upper left corner.

Which is when I realize that it's the flag of the Republic of the Marshall Islands.

Which is the last thing I need right now.

"Hello, everyone," Dr. Melville says. "I'd like to invite a very special student down to talk to you." He gestures up to the stands, to where I'm sitting. "A young man whose background and ambition are the very definition of the opportunity that Connaughton Academy offers to those with the willingness to advance in the world . . ." He pauses. "Alumni, parents, and faculty, please welcome William Shea."

The applause is thunderous.

"What is this?" I mutter, rising up slowly on knees that don't seem to be working quite right, and make my way down the aisle toward the field.

As I walk past Andrea, I feel her reach up and swat me on the butt. I look around at her.

"Did you do this?" I ask.

She grins. "Go get 'em, tiger."

TWENTY-FOUR

MANY OF YOU MAY NOT KNOW," DR. MELVILLE IS SAYing as I make my way out onto the field, "that Mr. Shea comes to us from halfway around the world, hailing from a remote Pacific Island called Ebeye."

From out in the crowd, I hear a single cackling laugh. I don't have to look up to know that it's Brandt. I can tell he's grinning at me. Dr. Melville ignores the distraction and presses dutifully on.

"I received an email last week from another student asking if Mr. Shea could come up and speak to all of us today about his homeland, about some of the ongoing difficulties that they've been facing for the past fifty years since the government began testing nuclear bombs in the Marshall Islands." Dr. Melville's voice becomes solemn. "The student who wrote that email is here with us today, and I'd like to invite her down as well." Turning, he gestures up to the stands again. "Andrea Dufresne?"

More applause. Andrea glides down on it like a pageant queen on a parade float of destiny. "Thank you, Dr. Melville." She takes the microphone from him and gives me a quick glance out of the corner of her eye—and now I don't even know her angle. I've clearly been snookered so smoothly that

I didn't even realize it was happening, but I don't even know what else Andrea has up her sleeve.

"As many of you know," she says, "I'm a scholarship student myself. My parents were U.S. aid workers who lost their lives in the Balkans. I'm attending Connaughton thanks to the gracious support of the administration and alumni endowments. But when I heard about the obstacles that Will has had to overcome after the tragic death of both of his parents—who were flying medicine to an orphanage when their lives were so unexpectedly cut short—and the way that his community came together to send him here for school, well . . . I knew that I'd found not just a kindred spirit for myself, but an inspiration for all of us." She looks up at the flag. "Will, can you tell us a little bit about your country's flag?"

As she leans over to give me the microphone. I cup my hand over it, still smiling, and whisper, "I will *so* get you for this."

"Sure," she whispers, and smiles back.

I look up. The crowd has fallen silent, their eyes on me. Over my shoulder I can hear the flag flapping and popping in the breeze.

"This flag . . ." I begin, and take a breath, wondering why I never bothered to learn what "my" flag represented. "Of course, the deep blue symbolizes the ocean. These orange and white stripes you see here are the symbol of hope and . . . ah, good stewardship. And the sun in the corner represents . . . uh . . . the sun. Which is extremely bright in my country. And hot."

I glance over at Dr. Melville, but he's not smiling anymore.

He actually looks a little confused. Walking over, he takes the microphone from my hand and turns to look at the flag.

"Excuse me, Mr. Shea," he says, "but when I wrote my doctoral thesis on the Marshall Islands, it was my understanding that the twenty-four-pointed star in the corner is a representation of the twenty-four municipal districts. And the orange and white bands symbolize the Ratak and Ralik chains?" He turns back to me, extending the microphone. "Isn't that right?"

"Actually," I say, "no."

His eyebrows hike up halfway to his hairline. *"No?"*

"No. Because, you see, the flag was actually redefined last year. All those symbols mean different things now. The government changed it."

"I'm sorry," he says. "They *changed* it?"

I nod. "They took a vote, and the people decided they wanted it to mean something different. It was called the, uh, Cultural Transition Initiative. It's really fascinating, in fact. You should read up on it."

"I'll be sure to do that," he says, giving me back the microphone and taking a step back, looking more bewildered than ever. Up in the stands, people are beginning to lose interest, and I realize that halftime is going to be over soon but not quite soon enough. As the band marches out onto the field, Andrea steps forward and takes the microphone from me.

"As a special treat," she says, "Will has volunteered to sing us his country's national anthem, 'Forever Marshall Islands.'" She turns to me. "Ready, Will?"

"Actually, I don't think—"

"Our marching band has already learned the music. Don't leave us hanging."

I take her hand. "Only if you join me."

"I don't know the words."

"Just follow my lead," I say, as the band strikes up a stately tune that sounds oddly similar to "The Star-Spangled Banner" but that must, in fact, be the anthem of my homeland far away. When the moment seems right, I take in a deep breath and begin to sing, with as much gusto as I can manage:

> *Oh, Marshall Islands,*
> *My home across the sea.*
> *You are a very small island,*
> *Extremely difficult to see.*
> *Most maps don't include you;*
> *You're not on any chart.*
> *But oh, Marshall Islands—*
> *You're always in my heart.*

Somewhere across the field, Dr. Melville is shouting something over the music. He doesn't have a microphone, but I can read lips well enough to know what he's saying: "Those aren't the lyrics!" And he's right, of course—if the person who'd written the actual Marshall Islands national anthem were here now, he'd probably be ready to have me dragged away in chains for a year of cultural awareness training, which, quite frankly, would've come in really handy *before* I'd started telling people I was from there.

I turn to Andrea, who—against almost insurmountable odds—has managed to keep a straight face, and now she joins me in repeating the ridiculous words that I just made up on the spot. We're going faster now, upping the tempo of the song. Still belting out the lyrics, she spins around to the band conductor, grabs his baton, and swings both arms up in the air, kicking the drum majorettes into triple time as the rest of the band struggles frantically to keep up. Cymbals crash, and the stately anthem accelerates into a Dixieland swing. Our mascot, Colby the Connaughton Cougar, has run out onto the field and starts doing backflips in front of the band.

"You're not on any *chart*..." Now the lyrics come out sounding like some alternate-universe combination of pep rally and New Orleans funeral. "You're always in my *heart*..." Andrea pivots around to face the stands. "Come on, everybody," she shouts, "on your feet! You know this part!"

I look out and I'm amazed at what I see. The music *has* done something to the students and faculty and alumni, and now they're on their feet, singing along while Andrea coaches them through it. As Colby the Cougar executes a perfect handspring in front of us, I lean in again and join Andrea for the third chorus. Encouraged by Colby and the response of the Connaughton crowd, the band is now doing some crazy drumline moves that I'm pretty sure nobody's seen before, and a few of them grab the flag and wave it high in the air. Dr. Melville is now trying to push his way through to grab the microphone, but he can't get through the majorettes and the color guard. Meanwhile, Andrea and I are bringing it home.

"But oh, Marshall Islands," we finish together, "you're always in my heart!" And when the drums and trumpets thunder to a crescendo, the crowd erupts in a roar of spontaneous applause. I realize I'm smiling, and Andrea is too, and I can't tell if either of us really means it, but at the moment it doesn't matter. For the moment I've forgotten about Gatsby. I'm back in my element, doing what I do best, faking it like a champ, and it feels *good*.

"Thank you," Andrea says to the crowd, sounding a little out of breath. Her cheeks are bright red and her eyes are reflecting tiny darts of the early-November sunlight, and when she looks at me, the smile on her face is genuine. "You guys are the best." She grabs my hand again. "Which is why I know you're going to be excited when you hear this next part—one week from today, next Saturday, the head of the Ebeye Children's Health Clinic is going to be here at Connaughton to receive the funds to build a new orphanage on the island that Will Shea calls home."

"Wait . . ." I stare at her.

My thoughts go spinning in a corkscrew, fluttering to the bottom of my brainpan. Meanwhile, Andrea gestures to the band, and they reach down to unfurl a new banner, which reads: CONNAUGHTON ACADEMY SUPPORTS THE ORPHANS OF EBEYE!

"Many of our alumni have already made some extremely generous pledges," she says, "including one special pledge from a very special individual that we all know very well." Turning to the stands, she flicks the hair from her eyes. "Brandt Rush has graciously volunteered to donate fifty thousand dollars."

Applause. Cheers.

I turn to stare at Andrea again.

Just in time to see her lean in toward me to whisper in my ear.

"Game over, Shea," she murmurs, still smiling. "You lose."

TWENTY-FIVE

WHOA," THE TWENTY-SOMETHING GUY BEHIND THE monitor says admiringly. It's Iron Mike Mullen, one of the smalltimers that Uncle Roy brought up from Boston. The screen in front of him reads: *Connaughton Alumni for Ebeye.* "These people already have their own website."

I don't say anything. I've got my books spread out on the floor of our rented office space in Lowell, and for some reason that even I don't understand, I'm trying to study for a U.S. Diplomacy midterm while everybody else scrambles to find a way to salvage the con. Roy's sitting in the corner, stewing in a robust marinade of his own silence. He's got a good reason for being furious with me. I wasn't up-front with him about my bet with Andrea, and now, within a week, we're going to lose everything.

"Why can't we just go ahead with the scam?" Dad asks him.

"Because she'll tip off the mark," Roy says abruptly. "Haven't you been paying attention?" He swivels to glare at me. "That was the deal, wasn't it, William? The part that you didn't feel compelled to tell us? First one to fifty thousand wins? If she gets the Rush kid to pay out first, she ruins it for us."

"So what?" Dad shrugs and glances at Rhonda, who's sitting across from him, painting her fingernails. "So we take the girl out of the equation."

"Take her out . . . ?" I look at him. "Wait a second, what are you talking about? You can't—"

"Look," Dad says. "Let's get something straight. I know you have a soft spot for this girl, but I'm not allowing your little high school crush ruin our shot at two million bucks. If you think I'm going to let that happen, you're reading all the wrong books."

"It's got nothing to do with—"

"I don't care. I'm just saying, we take care of her."

Uncle Roy gets up and walks over to Dad. "What are you saying?"

"We send her packing," Dad says. "This is *our* deal. She wants to keep trying to fleece these millionaires for some made-up charity for a bunch of orphans, then that's her thing, but we're going to finish this."

"She'll tip off Brandt."

Dad shakes her head. "Then we don't give her that chance. We shut her down. Hard."

I stand up. "No."

"*No?*" He's getting that look now, darkness gathering across his face, falling over his eyes like the shadow of an object dropping fast. Seeing him like this gives me a bright coppery taste in my mouth that I associate with early childhood, the old familiar panic of powerlessness.

"Nobody's getting hurt," I say. "This isn't that kind of deal."

Dad moves right up close to me and stands directly in front of my face. Whiskey fumes stream invisibly from his nostrils. Everybody else in the office has stopped what he's doing to watch us. When Dad speaks, the words are little more than a snarl.

"Listen to me, junior. I taught you everything you know about the long con. We're all here because of what you promised us."

"No," I say, "you're here because you're a drunk and you're too irresponsible to make it on your own. I didn't want you here. Ever since you showed up, all you've done is ruin everything."

"Easy, boy." Dad's voice is ominously quiet. "Don't say things that you're gonna regret when we get back home to Trenton."

"I'm never going back to Trenton," I say, and for a long second, the words just hang there.

"What?"

"You heard me." My heart is pounding and I force myself to stand my ground. "I can fix this situation myself. I worked too hard to get where I am now. This is my life. I'm not going back."

Dad shoves me backwards. I don't see it coming, and the thrust propels me into an empty desk, where I whack my skull on the arm of a chair before hitting the ground. I start to shake off the pain, but Dad is lunging again, landing on top of me with his fist cocked back, and it's only because of Uncle Roy pulling him off that I don't catch his knuckles across the bridge of my nose.

Roy's old, but he's tough. He tosses Dad aside like a sack of dirty laundry. Dad starts to stand up, and Roy fixes him with a look that says: *Try it.*

"You come at me like that again, Roy," Dad says in a low voice, "you better bring a gun."

"Shut your cake hole," Uncle Roy says. "Nobody's doing anything with *guns.*" He pronounces that last word with the disdain of a man who regards such things as the last resort of the desperate and incompetent, guys too knuckleheaded to handle themselves any other way. Pausing to collect himself, Roy tucks in his shirt, pulls out a comb, and runs it through his hair. "Okay, now, listen. Everybody just breathe. We all know the situation isn't optimal. That doesn't mean it's hopeless." He points at me. "William, your dad's right about one thing. You got us into this, you're going to get us out."

"Damn straight," Dad says.

Roy holds up a hand. "Today's Monday. Now, my understanding is that the Rush kid isn't writing his fifty-grand check for the orphans of Ebeye until Saturday, am I right?"

I nod. "That's right."

"So all we have to do is get him back here in this office, cash in hand, sometime before then."

"He wants another ten-thousand-dollar trial run," I say.

Uncle Roy shakes his head. "That's impossible—we're out of time. You need to convince him that if he's going to take down McDonald, then he needs to place that big bet before Saturday."

"How am I supposed to do that?"

"Hey, you're a smart kid," Uncle Roy says cheerfully, gesturing at the textbooks and notes I've got scattered around the floor. "You'll figure something out."

TWENTY-SIX

I WAKE UP IN THE MORNING FEELING EXHAUSTED. I DIDN'T sleep well at all—I know it's my imagination, but I swear I can feel Dr. Melville's counterfeit Bible tucked under my box spring like some fractured fairy tale version of the princess and the pea. Imaginary or not, the lump wouldn't bother me so much if it didn't remind me of Gatsby, who I haven't heard from since the lacrosse game. Meanwhile, it's seven a.m., and I've got a U.S. Diplomacy midterm in an hour that I couldn't feel less prepared for. I grab a coffee from the Starbucks in the arts center, take a big gulp of French roast, and head off to class.

The exam goes even worse than I had feared. From the moment I look down at the essay question on Wilson's Fourteen Points, my mind goes blank. People around me are already scribbling fiercely, the room full of the sound of scratching pencils, while I spend an hour staring at the empty page, wondering how on earth I ever thought I could fit in here.

With five minutes left on the clock, I toss the blue book onto the teacher's desk and walk out the door.

I'm sitting in the dining hall, staring out the window, when Gatsby takes a seat next to me.

"Will, we need to talk."

"Look," I say, "it's okay. You don't need to say anything."

"Just let me explain, okay?"

I look at her and nod.

"I've never been invited to Homecoming before," Gatsby says. "When you invited me, I was really excited. I had been hoping you'd ask me."

"So . . . ?"

She closes her eyes, opens them again. "There was this boy back on the Vineyard. His name was Del James. He was a baseball player, and I had this huge crush on him. We had this middle school Valentine's Day dance, and he invited me. At first I couldn't believe it—it seemed too good to be true. My friends all told me that I had to say yes."

I don't say anything. I can already see where this is going and I don't want to hear it, but it's too late.

"I got a new dress and new shoes," Gatsby says, "and my dad paid for me to get my hair done at this fancy salon in Boston. I remember looking in the mirror and feeling so grown up." She stops and swallows and looks up at me. "But when I got to the dance, Del just looked at me and started laughing. He told me he'd only done it on a dare. His friends had bet him that he wouldn't ask out the ugliest girl in the class. They all thought it was hilarious. The worst part—" Gatsby stops and takes in a little breath. "He convinced my own friends to encourage me to go. *Everybody* was in on it except for me."

"Gatsby," I say, and my mouth feels as dry as sand, "I'm sorry."

"No," she says, "it's not your fault. As I was getting ready

the other night, I just kept thinking, *What if it happens again?*"
She reaches over and touches my hand. "But you're different,
Will. I see that."

I can't look at her.

"I know how well things are going for you," she says.
"With Rush making that donation to your orphanage, and all
the increased awareness that's going on about the situation in
Ebeye, you've got to be so excited."

"It's not that big a deal."

"Yes it is." She holds up her hand to stop me from interrupt-
ing. "Will, look at me. You've seen poverty and privation that
none of us can imagine. You grew up in the poorest area of the
Pacific, and your parents literally gave their lives to serve others.
You've got every right to be bitter and discouraged, but instead
you're decent and optimistic and fair. When I think about it,
you're the perfect antidote to the Brandt Rushes of the world."

"Yeah," I mumble. "It's great."

"It *is*," she says. "And okay, I know Andrea's the one who
initiated the fundraiser, and it's exactly the sort of project that
she'd undertake just to pad her college application, but with
the money that's coming in to help your island—"

"It's not my island."

"Well, yes, obviously it's not *your* island, but it is your
home. You grew up there, and—"

"You're not listening to me," I say, a lot more sharply than I
had intended. *"It's not my home."*

Across the table, Gatsby regards me peculiarly. "What are
you saying?"

The silence between us stretches out for an unreal amount of time. Far off, I hear the clink of silverware and ice. Deep inside, I can already feel something rising into my throat. It's sharp and angular and unpleasant, and that's when I realize that it's the truth. A cowardly voice pipes up from inside me.

If you tell her this, you'll ruin everything.

Too late for that now.

"What if I told you" — I take in a breath and let it out, making myself look her in the eye — "that I wasn't really from some island in the Pacific?"

And everything stops. Gatsby blinks and shakes her head a little. "What?"

"What if I told you that I'm really just a kid from New Jersey, and this whole thing about my parents being missionaries and dying in a plane crash was just a story that I made up so that I could go to school here?"

"I don't understand." Now Gatsby's just staring at me. "You're saying you're *not* from the Marshall Islands?"

"I'm from Trenton, New Jersey. My real name is Billy Humbert. This is the third school that I've sneaked into in two years."

"You're from . . . New Jersey," she repeats slowly, like she's just trying to get the facts straight in her own mind. "How did you . . ."

"I forged my transcripts. Faked my letters of recommendation. Hacked into the school's database and gave myself a whole new history." I pause. "Gatsby, look, I know it was wrong. I never wanted to lie to you about all of this, I swear."

She's already pushing herself back, standing up, leaving her tray on the table. She doesn't say anything. The look on her face is the worst part. The way that she just keeps staring at me.

"Gatsby, wait."

But she's walking away. I go after her, following her out of the dining hall. "I can explain everything," I say, but that's just another lie, because no amount of explanation is going to excuse what I did or help her understand why, and it's far too late anyway.

Running around the corner, I almost collide with George the Kant-reading security guard.

"Shea," he says. "Come with me."

"Not right now."

"Right now." He reaches down and takes hold of my arm. "Dr. Melville wants to talk to you. He says it's important."

TWENTY-SEVEN

I'D NEVER BEEN UP TO THE PRESIDENT'S OFFICE. THE OUTER reception area is a large, two-hundred-year-old drawing room on the third floor of Connaughton's administration building. It's absolutely silent up here and smells so much like old money that you'd almost expect the hallway to be wallpapered with it. Rich brocade carpeting covers the hardwood floors, and stained-glass windows on both walls depict the illustrious history of the school from 1866 onward. When George leads me down the length of the room, I see Dr. Melville's secretary glance up and nod.

"He's inside," she says. "Go on in."

I look at George for some hint of what I'm walking into, although I suppose I already know. George, for his part, shows me no glimpse of what's going on behind those pale blue, philosophy-reading eyes.

"Thanks," I say.

Without a word, George opens the door and I step through it.

The inner office smells like pipe tobacco, rich and faintly cherry-scented. Its walls are lined with bookshelves, row upon row of dusty leather-bound hardcovers, the complete works of Shakespeare to John Updike to whatever guys such as Dr.

Melville read when they've exhausted the classics. Off to my right, a fire roars in a huge fieldstone hearth, with Dr. Melville's dog, Chaucer, sprawled on the rug in front of it, paws twitching from the depths of some rabbit-chasing dream.

"Mr. Humbert," Dr. Melville says. "That *is* your real name, isn't it?" He's seated behind a varnished oak slab of a desk that looks only slightly smaller than the state of Rhode Island, his broad shoulders and imperious head backlighted by the open window behind him. He points to a chair on the opposite side of the desk. "Sit."

"Sir—" I begin, because it seems like a decent place to start.

Dr. Melville holds up one hand. "Not a word. Not unless you have an attorney present. I assure you, you're going to need one."

I don't say anything. I just look over at Dr. Melville's dog stretched in front of the fire, dozing without the slightest notion of what's going on. Right now I'd happily trade places with him and spend the rest of my life at the end of a leash.

"After what happened on Saturday," Dr. Melville says, nodding at a stack of documents piled on his desk, "I started to look more closely at your transcripts. And your letters of recommendation. And your life. I'm sure you won't be surprised by the ease with which your web of lies began to unravel."

I don't say anything. I've been instructed to stay quiet and I'm determined to follow orders, at least in this one small aspect.

"What you've done here at Connaughton over the past weeks," Dr. Melville says, "is an embarrassment to yourself, to the board of directors, and to the reputation of this school. In my wildest dreams I can't imagine the circumstances under which you thought this was a good idea." He rises to his feet so fast that he sends his swivel chair rolling backwards, and it's the first time that I see just how angry he is. "Are you delusional? Do you have any idea the magnitude and implications of what you've done?"

I open my mouth and close it again, then reconsider. He seems to really want an answer. "Sir, I'm sorry."

"You're sorry. How wonderful." Dr. Melville glares at me thunderously from across the desk. "Thank you for that. You've humiliated me and left a permanent stain on the reputation of one of the finest preparatory schools in the country, and you're sorry."

I don't say anything.

"The police are on their way." He drops back into the chair and plants his elbows on the desk. "They'll be here in fifteen minutes. I've arranged for them to meet you outside the front gates, which is a small mercy, sparing us the additional indignity of seeing a Connaughton student led away in handcuffs." He looks at his watch. "I recommend that you spend the intervening time getting your things together."

"Sir . . ."

"Just out of my own morbid curiosity," he says, "exactly how long did you expect to keep up this charade? Obviously long enough to swindle our alumni into funding this fictitious orphanage of yours. Are you aware that they've already donated more than eighty thousand dollars to your so-called charity? *Eighty thousand,* with no sign of slowing down. Tell me, did you plan on running off with the money yourself or splitting it with Ms. Dufresne?"

Andrea—I hadn't even thought about her. Suddenly my tongue feels like it's glued to the roof of my mouth. This is my opportunity to rat her out, to expose her for the fraud that she is, and we'll both be thrown out of Connaughton. All I have to do is tell the truth and she's as dead as I am.

"Sir, Andrea Dufresne . . ." I swallow, looking down at the floor and back up at him. "She had nothing to do with it. She thinks I was telling the truth. This is all my fault."

Dr. Melville stares at me for a long moment, as if he doesn't know what to do with this information. Then he points to the door. Over on the rug before the fire, I see Chaucer lift his head ever so slightly as I pass, one eyebrow cocked to make sure he's not missing anything, before dropping his head back down and returning to doggy dreamland.

"Pack your bags, Mr. Humbert. Get out of my sight."

"Okay." Then I pause, as if a last-minute thought has just occurred to me. "Oh, by the way. Speaking of humiliation, it's too bad about the Gutenberg."

Dr. Melville glares at me. *"What?"*

"I'm just curious. When your father sold it to the school in exchange for your getting a full ride, did he know it was a fake?"

Dr. Melville says nothing. His mouth sags open, just a little. All the color drains from his face, leaving it dead-white, and I can see the muscles twitching in his throat as he struggles to breathe.

"You." Dr. Melville manages to recover a little bit of his composure. "You stole that Bible."

I shake my head. "No, sir."

"I'll search your room. I'll find it. I'll have you arrested. You'll go to jail."

"Considering what I know about you, Dr. Melville, I don't think any additional publicity would be wise at this point, do you?" I wait a moment for that to sink in. "Now, I will offer you a deal."

"*You . . .*" Now he's apoplectic, trembling, a vein pulsing in the side of his head. "You'll make *me* a deal?"

I nod. "Let me stay here at Connaughton, and I won't tell anyone how you paid for your education."

"You're insane."

"Sorry." I spread my hands, palms upturned in the universal gesture of someone who's not hiding anything. "That's my best offer. Otherwise, I can't guarantee you'll ever see it again."

Dr. Melville sizzles. He stews. He squirms in his seat, and a vein in his temple throbs like it's about to bust loose and run a 5K. Those last words hang there for a long moment, until he reaches over, picks up the phone, and dials. "Yes, Sergeant, it's Dr. Melville at Connaughton Academy." Throughout the whole conversation, his eyes never leave mine. "There's been a misunderstanding. No, we won't be needing the officers any longer."

And he hangs up.

"You've made the right choice," I say.

Dr. Melville's hands are still trembling slightly. He looks like he's about to come vaulting over the desk to grab me by the throat. In a small, tight voice, he says: "You're going to regret this, Mr. Humbert. I can guarantee that."

"Maybe so." I shrug. "But considering what's at stake, you've got a lot more to lose than I do, don't you think?" Just in case he's still missing the point, I count off on my fingers. "The school's integrity. Your personal reputation. Your job here. You really want people finding out the truth about any of this stuff?"

He's still just sitting there clenching his fists as I walk out of the office, down the hall, and outside into the afternoon light. Then I start to run. I've got so much to think about that I don't know where to start. First, though, I've got to get back to my room and hide the Gutenberg somewhere more secure than inside my box spring. No doubt Dr. Melville's probably already on the phone to security, sending them over to my room to shake it down from top to bottom, and that includes flipping my mattress.

Sprinting across the lawn in front of the admin building, I make my way toward the tall oaks on the side of the quad. A brightly painted banner hangs between them: CONNAUGHTON ACADEMY SUPPORTS THE ISLAND OF EBEYE AND THE MARSHALL ISLANDS!

The clock tower strikes ten with its resonant chimes as I cut through the crowds. There are students hurrying, late for class. I run faster, pushing between them, no longer noticing the looks that I'm getting. My dorm is up ahead, just around the corner. I can make it. I've got time.

That's when I see the security truck pulling up in front of my building. I stagger to a halt as George jumps out and goes through the door, no doubt headed right for my room. I can't move — I'm just standing there, trying to catch my breath.

Whatever I do now, it's too late.

Somewhere off to my right, a shadow emerges from behind a tree.

And that's when the fist comes flying out of nowhere, knocking me into darkness.

TWENTY-EIGHT

Y OU WANT A COFFEE?" BRANDT RUSH ASKS.

When I open my eyes, I'm sprawled on my back on the floor of his triple-size suite in Crowley House, and my right cheekbone is throbbing and numb where Carl hooked into it with a fist the size of a parking meter. I smell freshly brewed coffee, something dark and rich and European. Lifting my head, I look around. I've seen this place only when it was full-on Casino Night, and now the room looks huge and silent and weirdly anonymous, like a hotel room. The green velvet blackjack and poker tables rise up on either side of me, and Brandt just stands there, looking down at me, sipping coffee from a Las Vegas mug.

"I'm telling you, this is good stuff." He takes another sip. "I brew freshly ground beans every morning, get 'em flown up from Guatemala each week." Without looking over, he snaps his fingers at Carl, who's sitting at the blackjack table, reading a textbook. "Get him a cup of coffee."

Carl looks up. "I'm studying, Brandt."

"What, trigonometry? Why bother?" Brandt snaps his fingers again. "Coffee, now. Let's go."

Carl starts to stand up.

"I'm fine, Carl," I say, and look back at Brandt. "What am I doing here?"

"I heard Melville called you into his office, having done some research into your file. Andrea told me all about your 'history' after that fiasco at the Homecoming game on Saturday. I just wanted to make sure that Melville hasn't figured out what's really going on."

I rub my jaw. "And that required my getting punched in the face?"

"Nothing personal. I just needed to get your attention."

"Can I ask you something?" I rise to my feet. "Why are you bothering to donate all this money to the orphanage, if you know I'm a fraud?"

"It was Andrea's idea, something about how it's going to look on her Harvard application. Besides, if you get tossed out now, I'll never get a chance to nail McDonald. So this way, everybody wins."

"Thanks."

"Hey, what are friends for?" Brandt says, but it's not really a question. "This Friday, we'll do one more test run for ten thousand just to make sure there aren't any more surprises. If that works, I'll talk to my accountant and get the full two million."

I can't think of any way to persuade him that this needs to happen sooner without blowing the whole deal. "And you're still donating the fifty thousand to Ebeye?"

Brandt shrugs. "Sure — why not? You gotta give back somehow, right?" He picks up a deck of cards and starts shuffling them absently, doing small tricks with his fingers while he talks. "Anyhow, fifty grand is nothing in my family—it's like a rounding error. It's not like *I'm* gonna notice either way. It's probably enough for those poor losers to build a bunch of mud huts or whatever it is they live in down there, you know what I'm saying?" He smirks. "Not that *you'd* know."

"Where is Andrea, anyway?"

"Funny." Brandt looks up. "I was gonna ask you that same question. She missed our breakfast date. That's not like her."

"How long has she been out of touch?"

"A couple hours."

I think of my dad saying, *We take the girl out of the equation,* and turn to walk out. Carl is standing by the door, blocking the exit.

"Where are you going?" Brandt asks.

"I'll be back in touch with you about Friday," I say, and squeeze past Carl through the doorway. "I'll let you know if I see Andrea."

"You do that," Brandt says.

It's too late to go back to my room for the Gutenberg, but I've got something more important to take care of now.

By the time I hit the hallway, I'm running.

TWENTY-NINE

AN HOUR LATER, I'M STANDING OUTSIDE DAD'S ROOM AT the Motel 6 with my ear to the door. There's a DO NOT DISTURB sign hanging on the knob, and I can hear the TV blasting inside.

I pound on the door and wait, but there's no answer. I pound harder, then turn and go back up the hallway to where a housekeeping cart sits outside another room.

"Excuse me?"

The housekeeper looks at me warily.

"My dad forgot to give me the key," I say. "Could you by any chance let me in?"

She walks back up the hall, pulls out a master key, and unlocks the room for me, stepping aside while I go in and let the door shut behind me.

The place is a Chernobyl of bachelor living run amok. Fast food wrappers clutter the unmade bed, and Dad's clothes, dirty and clean, are scattered across the table and onto the floor. A sock dangles from a lampshade. There's a half-empty bottle of whiskey on the table and the TV is louder than ever. I reach down to switch it off, and that's when I hear the noises from inside the bathroom.

I walk over and look inside, pulling aside the shower curtain.

Andrea's sitting there, tied to a chair inside the bathtub, her wrists and ankles wrapped in black electrician's tape with what looks like about a half roll of it around her mouth. When she sees me, her eyes get really big and she starts to thrash around, stomping her feet on the floor and jerking her head up and down.

"Take it easy," I say. "I have to find something to cut through this tape." I go back out to the main room and dig through Dad's suitcase until I find a pocketknife tucked into an outside compartment, then bring it back into the bathroom. "Hold still, okay?" She grunts and snorts and rolls her eyes. "Sorry. This is going to hurt." I peel the tape off her mouth. "Are you all right?"

"What do you think?"

"Nice to see you too."

"Well, what are you waiting for? Aren't you going to cut me loose?"

"Just calm down, and—"

"After your stupid father and that floozy girlfriend of his kidnapped me and taped me to a chair?" She jerks her arms and shoulders back and forth. "Cut this off me!"

"Okay—just try not to move."

"You think I have a choice? I've been sitting here for three hours—I'm claustrophobic, and I'm going out of my mind in this tiny space!"

"Just hold on a second—I have to think."

"What is there to think about? Cut me loose!"

I glance down. There's a sheet of paper sticking out of her sweatshirt pocket, and I reach down and pull it out.

The letterhead reads: EBEYE CHILDREN'S HEALTH CLINIC, REPUBLIC OF MARSHALL ISLANDS. And below it:

> *Dear Ms. Dufresne:*
>
> *Thank you for your great kindness in flying our family to Connaughton Academy to receive the money that you have collected for our new orphanage. My wife and I cannot begin to express our gratitude for what you have done for the orphans of our country.*
>
> *We are looking forward to seeing you soon.*
>
> *God bless you.*
>
> *Nathan Stanley, MD*
> *Director, Ebeye Children's Health Clinic,*
> *Republic of Marshall Islands*

"Wow," I say. "This is really convincing." I hand back the fax. "Nice job on the letterhead—it actually looks real."

"That's because it is, you idiot," Andrea says.

"Wait—" And now I'm just staring at her as she's holding up the paper. "This guy is really coming here?"

"After Brandt told me about your online poker plan," she says, "I had to step up my game, make sure I got his money before you did. Stanley and his wife and kids are flying in tomorrow from Ebeye for a long weekend. There's going to be reporters and TV news crews up from Boston to cover the whole event. The alumni of Connaughton are going to present him with one of those big checks with the name of the clinic on it and everything—it's up to almost a hundred thousand now. Of course, the actual money will be going into my pocket, but hey, I don't think I'll be hanging around to finish the semester anyway."

"But I thought our bet was about who got to stay."

"Come off it, Humbert. People like us don't belong here and we both know it. You're telling me you were actually planning on sticking around if *you* won?"

"Andrea . . ." Suddenly I can't move. This whole thing has gone too far.

"Hey, don't look at me. You're the one who never bothered to learn your country's national anthem." Her eyes narrow. "But I think Gatsby is starting to suspect something."

"Gatsby already knows," I say.

"What did you tell her?"

"The truth." I start backing away.

"Wait—" Andrea starts thrashing around in the chair. If she's not careful, she's going to fall over. "Will, what are you doing?" she shouts. "You can't leave me here like this! Get this tape off me!"

"I can't right now," I say, still backing away. "If I cut you loose, Dad will know something's up. I'm sorry, but if you just hang in there, I think we can both get what we want."

"That's impossible!" she shouts. "What I want is for you to die a slow, painful death!"

"I'm sorry—I'll be back, I promise. My dad is harmless." *I think,* I add silently.

"Will, you idiot!" Stepping out of the bathroom, I hear the chair legs rattling around in the tub. "I'll kill you for this!"

She's still yelling at me as I duck out the motel door.

THIRTY

BACK AT CONNAUGHTON, I MAKE MY WAY ACROSS CAMPUS and to my dorm. My room has definitely been searched and my stuff has been rummaged through — clothes, books, and papers strewn everywhere as if by some clumsy-fingered hurricane — but when I crawl underneath my bed, the Gutenberg is still there, taped up snugly inside my box spring.

I pull it out and walk to the library, carrying it up to the circulation desk.

"Gatsby."

She turns around and looks at me, her face blank, as I place the Bible on the desk in front of her. She doesn't say anything.

"I just came here to say I'm really sorry. I was so wrong. I never meant —" I stop myself, cutting short the urge to somehow justify or explain. "I did a really crappy thing by lying to you."

She still doesn't say anything. I've stood in front of suspicious cops and angry gamblers and hostile caseworkers, but those were all situations that I'd eventually managed to weasel out of or avoid completely. The only way out of this one is to go through it. I take a deep breath.

"And the worst part is, I really like you. You're different from everybody else here."

"No," she says.

"What?"

"I said no." Gatsby shakes her head. "I'm not different," she says. "If I were, I wouldn't have been so eager to swallow your stupid, pathetic, made-up story."

"You trusted me," I say. "Faith is a good trait to have."

"Not in losers like you, it's not."

"Okay," I say, "valid point. But I just—"

"Stop, Will, okay? Just . . . *stop*." She's holding up both hands. "You've only been here a couple weeks, and it turns out now that I never really knew you at all. Honestly, I'd prefer to just leave it at that."

I look at her. And now I know what I have to do.

"I need to show you something," I tell her.

She turns away, shaking her head. "What makes you think—"

"Please." I catch her eye. "I'll be back." I look down at my hand and see that it's resting on the Bible. "I swear."

Two hours later, we're standing by the helipad at the corner of campus while a high-pitched whine gets louder, the leaves and branches whipping around us. As a helicopter descends, there's too much noise to speak, but that's probably a good thing. The conversation at this point would undoubtedly be a little awkward anyway.

"Whose helicopter is that?" Gatsby shouts.

"It belongs to the Rush family."

"What's it doing here?"

That's a more complicated answer. Essentially it involved my going back to Brandt and telling him that I needed to borrow his family chopper and pilot for the afternoon and evening. I made it sound like our scam depended on it and I didn't leave him a choice, and Brandt hardly even hesitated. I've discovered that when dealing with the very rich, reasonable requests only make them suspicious. Ask for the moon and you're golden.

"Where are we going?" Gatsby shouts as she climbs inside.

"Just get in, and—"

"Don't tell me to trust you."

I don't say anything, just climb in behind her, and we strap the harnesses over our shoulders and laps. We're already climbing, rising up over the trees and the statue of Lancelot Connaughton, and as the chopper tilts, I look down at the grounds from an angle that I've never seen before, watching it shrink below me, first the lacrosse field and the dorms, then the pond and, farther out, the Atlantic coastline, until it's all gone beneath the orange and red blanket of New England foliage.

"We're heading south," Gatsby says, gazing out the window. "What am I supposed to be seeing?"

"Nothing yet."

She looks at me suspiciously for a moment, huddled on her side of the seat, as far away from me as she can get. I don't want to tell her any more because I'm afraid I'll change my mind, even now. I promised myself I wouldn't go back, ever. The truth is, my palms are already starting to sweat.

An hour later, we're crossing high above Manhattan, still heading south. When I look down again, the skyscrapers have been replaced by clusters of low buildings, warehouses and factories along the Delaware River. Heavy manufacturing. Urban enterprise zones. Neighborhoods of public housing. The world couldn't be more different from the one we just left behind. As the helicopter skims lower and lands on top of an abandoned warehouse, I can already see the sign on the Lower Free Bridge, and I hear her reading the words out loud.

"Trenton Makes," Gatsby reads, *"the World Takes."* She looks at me. "What are we doing here, Will?"

My voice is unsteady. I still can't quite believe I'm doing this.

"I wanted you to see where I'm from," I tell her.

She looks out the window. I can hear sirens from somewhere across the river, and the sound of traffic, and that's how I know it.

I'm home.

THIRTY-ONE

WE WALK FOR FIVE BLOCKS WITHOUT SAYING ANY-thing.

It's late afternoon, edging toward dusk and already getting dark on Parker Avenue, where the twilight seems to settle across the river like a dirty blanket. Immediately I feel all my old instincts coming back, a kind of heightened predator/prey awareness that creeps its way up my spine and tightens the skin across my scalp. I really don't want to be here. From this point forward, I know every crack in the sidewalk, every broken parking meter and ripped-out pay phone. Walking along, I keep my hands in my pockets because they're shaking a little and I don't want Gatsby to see. I can hear a baby crying from one of the buildings up the street. We stop in front of a three-story walkup with a fire escape hanging crookedly off the side.

"This is where I used to live," I tell Gatsby. "After my mom died. My mom and dad used to run the wedding-planner scam from an apartment across the river, but the cops shut us down."

Gatsby looks at me. "What's a wedding-planner scam?"

"Pretty much what it sounds like. You pick up the Sunday paper and read the engagement announcements and go around visiting couples, offering to do the wedding, the pictures, the flowers, the whole thing. They write you a check for a deposit, and you skip out with it."

"You actually did that to people?" Gatsby asks. "Took their savings away?"

"For a while, yeah." I hear sirens again, this time coming closer, and have to remind myself they're not for me—I don't have to look back or walk faster. "See that church?" I point past a parking lot enshrouded with a chainlink fence and a big sign reading NO LOITERING. "Dad and I went there right after my mom died."

"You went to church?"

"Not exactly," I say. "Dad and I sold hymnals to the priest. Except there really weren't any hymnals to sell." I shrugged. "I was nine years old at the time. It was the first time I remember lying to somebody's face."

"And they just gave you the money?"

"That's right."

"And you took it."

"You'd be surprised what people will believe when it comes from a kid." I point to a bar up on the corner. "See that place? Last year, we hustled a man out of five thousand bucks. It was his retirement money, probably everything he had in savings. He thought he was buying a time-share in the Outer Banks. I never saw him again."

"Will," Gatsby says slowly, "I get what you're doing, but I really don't think I need to know this . . ."

"It's not fun for me either," I say. "But I need you to know who I am."

We keep walking. After a while, we stop at an intersection, and Gatsby turns around, looking back at the old neighborhood. I can feel her trying to decide if this is just another angle that I'm playing, and I decide not to say anything. Down the block, the wind has begun to pick up, and it feels like it's getting colder by the second. Somewhere behind a fence, a dog keeps barking and barking. It sounds angry, hungry, or both. I can smell the chemicals across the river, and more than anything that takes me back to where I least want to be.

"I don't understand," she says. "Why did you bring me here?"

There's a rattle of metal off to the left. I feel a hot surge of adrenaline pulse through my arms. Somebody steps out of the alleyway in front of us—a tall, almost skeletally skinny guy in a hooded sweatshirt—and stares at me for a long second.

"You," he says.

I look back at him. "Richie?"

"Billy." The guy grins, then cackles happily, sticking out his hand for a fist-bump and a hug. "Good to see you, man! I didn't know you were back! Yo, Lisa, look who it is."

A woman in cornrows and a leather jacket comes around the corner, pushing a baby stroller, and gives me a shy smile. "Billy Humbert? What are you doing back here?" She glances at Richie. "It's been forever." Her eyes flash over to Gatsby while the baby in the stroller starts crying. "You brought a friend with you?"

"Rich, Lisa, this is—"

"G," Gatsby interrupts, holding out her hand, which Richie shakes. "I'm . . . a friend from school."

"Nice to meet you," Lisa says, reaching down to pick up the baby and rock her on her shoulder. "Billy and us go way back, don't we? Since he was growing up in the South Ward, and that was way back in the day."

Gatsby looks at the baby. "Your daughter is beautiful."

"Thanks," Lisa says. "Her name's Corrine. You wanna hold her?"

"I . . . uh—" That's as far as Gatsby gets before Lisa thrusts the baby into her arms, still crying. Lisa looks at me while Gatsby tries rocking Corrine, bouncing her on her shoulder. "How you been, honey?"

"I'm all right," I say, which is about as far from the truth as I can get. "Just came around to say hello, see how things were back in the neighborhood."

"Going to see your old man?" Rich asks, and I can tell from the way he says it that there's more to the story already. On Gatsby's shoulder, the baby's crying louder now, but Richie keeps talking, raising his voice to be heard over the wails. "Last time I saw him, he looked pretty rough. He still living in that place above the market?"

I shrug. "Haven't seen him lately."

"Rich and I were just heading over to St. Luke's for some dinner," Lisa says. "You want to join us? They start serving at five."

Gatsby hands Corrine back to Lisa, and we make our way

up the street, past shuttered storefronts and darkened windows, heading for the church in the distance. When we get to St. Luke's, the line of people waiting on the sidewalk is already starting to move inside, and I can smell hot food and fresh coffee. Gatsby and I step in line, and she leans over to whisper in my ear.

"Will, isn't this the church that you said . . ."

I nod. At this point I have no idea what I'm doing here but it's too late to turn back now. Walking into the sanctuary, we each grab a styrofoam plate and join the long, slow shuffle of people, most of them men, most of them silent, heading for the long tables, where a mismatched group of college kids and suburban families are serving hot sausages, fresh fruit, coffee and bottled water, granola bars and yogurt. There are stacks of clean blankets, coats, and hats in boxes by the doors. It's about as far from the dining hall at Connaughton as I can imagine, but the familiarity of it cuts deep, like the smell of the river or the sirens on State Street.

Sitting down with Rich and Lisa, Gatsby and I find ourselves looking across the open room to the back, where a bald priest whom I recognize from a long time ago is talking to a couple guys wearing shirts from the local food bank. Lisa starts feeding Corrine, who's already got yogurt smeared across her face, while Rich looks over at Gatsby.

"So, what school you go to?"

Gatsby glances at me. "It's, ah, not around here."

"Billy?"

I turn around and see the priest standing behind me, and just like that, his name pops into my head.

"Father Tom."

"You're Billy Humbert, aren't you? You and your dad used to live up on Congress Avenue." It's not really a question, because I already know he knows me and remembers the twenty-five hundred dollars that the parish handed over, eight years earlier, for the hymnals that never arrived. I stare at him. His craggy face is creased with deep wrinkles, but his blue eyes are clear and sharp. "How's your old man doing, anyway?"

"I don't—" I swallow hard. "I don't really see him that much anymore," I say. Father Tom just keeps staring. It occurs to me that, in a really uncomfortable way, everything I've done up until now has led me to this moment.

Behind me, Gatsby is holding Richie and Lisa's little girl on her knee while she chats with another woman and her teenage son. From the corner of my eye, I see her stop what she's doing and turn her eyes toward me.

I look up at Father Tom.

"I just wanted to say"—I clear my throat—"I'm sorry. About what we did."

Father Tom just regards me. We have stolen money from this man's church, a lot of money, and there are plenty of things he could say at this moment—he'd be well within his rights to call the police and hold me here till they arrive—but in the end he just puts a hand on my shoulder. It's a heavy hand, but the weight of it feels reassuring somehow.

"It's good to see you again, Billy," he says. "Don't be a stranger."

Then he turns and walks away.

"What was *that* about?" Gatsby asks as we make our way back up State Street. Rich and Lisa have said their goodbyes at the corner, turning left and vanishing into the night, leaving the two of us alone.

"I'm not sure," I say.

"The priest just let you walk away. Even after what you did."

I nod. And then it occurs to me that Father Tom let me go *because* he knew what I did, even though I'm not exactly sure what that means or how I'd explain it to Gatsby—or even to myself. It seems to me that the things that we most need to be forgiven for are the offenses that are inarguably all our fault, the crimes that we can't possibly atone for. And I wonder if that's what people mean when they use the word *grace*. I open my mouth to try to put this into words, but then I stop.

Instead I just ask: "Are you cold?"

"I'm okay." Gatsby glances up into the darkness to the top of a building. "This is us," she says.

"Yeah."

We go inside and start up the stairs toward the roof.

As we fly home, Gatsby falls asleep beside me, her head resting on my shoulder as I stare out the window at the glassy black expanse of the Atlantic coastline. I'm tired—exhausted, really —but my mind refuses to slow down. Something's changed, and it all has to do with that moment when Father Tom let me walk away, forgiven and clean, for no good reason at all, except that I needed it. I just wish I knew what it meant.

As we land, I feel Gatsby stirring, lifting her head and sitting up, rubbing her eyes. "Mm," she says sleepily, and looks at me. "Are we back?"

Nodding, I help her to her feet and we step down out of the helicopter, then make our way across the darkened grounds as I walk her back to her room. The night smells like the ocean and dry leaves. The next snowstorm we get won't melt away so quickly. There's a sadness to it, a sense that fall is coming to an end, once and for all.

"Gatsby?"

She looks up at me sleepily.

"I almost forgot—I brought you something. I picked it up before Homecoming."

I reach deep into my coat pocket and hand her the package. It's still wrapped in the faded old map of the Pacific. "You can just ignore the wrapping paper."

She peels off the map and pulls out the copy of Hawthorne's *Twice-Told Tales*, turning it over slowly in her hands. "It's lovely," she says, and then passes it back to me. "But I can't accept this."

"Why not? It's the real deal."

"That's not why."

"Gatsby—"

"I need time, Will."

I nod, and she just gazes up at me for a moment before stepping inside her room. I turn around, heading back toward my dorm, when a car swerves up in front of me, so close I have to jump backwards to avoid being hit. That's when I realize that time is the one thing I don't have.

"Get in," Dad says.

The car smells like a distillery mixed with cigarette smoke. Rhonda's in the passenger seat, chuffing a Camel Light while playing Candy Crush on her phone, so I climb into the back, which still isn't far enough away from either of them. "What are you doing back here?"

"Shut up." From the driver's seat, Dad looks back, his face twisted with anger. The car is idling, and Dad is showing no signs of putting it into drive. "What happened to Andrea?"

"What are you talking about?"

"I got back to the motel room and she was gone."

Shaking my head, I give him my best blank look. "Am I supposed to know what you're talking about?"

Dad's right eyelid flutters and his lower lip droops down just slightly on that side, and for a second he looks like a man suffering a mild stroke. Then he manages to thrust his arm back over the seat, grabbing ahold of my collar. Since we're in a compact car, there's nowhere for me to go, and frankly, at this point I'm too tired to stop him. "The maid said she let you into my room. I know you were there. You cut her loose."

"Dad, seriously —"

"I warned you about this. If you queer this deal for me, you'll be sucking your turkey and cranberry sauce through a tube this year, you understand?"

"A lovely holiday sentiment," I tell him. "Can I go to bed now?"

Dad reaches out toward Rhonda with his right palm up, and she puts something in his hand. In the light from the dashboard, I see that it's a gun—a small black automatic. Dad looks down at it for a moment, and then his eyes flick back up to me. His voice has become very low now, almost inaudible, and there's something about his quiet tone that scares me more than any amount of yelling and screaming.

"You've been through a lot," he says. "I know. So far, I've given you the benefit of the doubt. But you're a big boy now, and I'm just telling you this, man to man." Raising the gun, he points it straight at my head. "If you or that smalltime grifter girlfriend of yours botch this for me, there will be repercussions, you understand?"

"You're going to shoot me now?" I'm trying to hide the quaver in my voice, with minimal success. "Seriously?"

"I *need* this score." The gun doesn't move. "Don't mess it up for me, Billy."

"You already did that yourself, a long time ago." I pull the door handle and step out. "Oh, and Dad?" I lower my head to glance back in at him. "Father Tom says hello."

I walk the rest of the way to my room without looking back.

THIRTY-TWO

I WAKE UP LATE THE NEXT MORNING TO THE SOUND OF squirrels chattering and squabbling outside my window. It's almost ten a.m. but it feels much later, and I roll over as thick fingers of daylight attempt to push their way under the curtains. The squabbling noises get louder, becoming progressively more animated and articulate, shaping themselves into words and sentences. Which means either Connaughton Academy has the most intelligent squirrels in the world, or . . .

. . . they aren't squirrels.

Pulling aside the curtain, I look out and see the Fox 25 TV news van parked across the lawn next to a platform with an empty podium and a microphone. There are several reporters out there already, along with mike booms and cameras, and a group of curious students has gathered outside a wood barricade.

This can't be good.

Somewhere in my dresser I find a clean set of clothes, and I brush my teeth and grab my coat before stepping out into the bright, cold morning air, which is when I see the new banner hanging from the trees overhead:

Oh no.

From up the road comes the loud roar of a diesel engine. I can already see an airport shuttle bus pulling up on the other side of the barricade, and the crowd steps back as the cameras surge forward with the instinctive feeding frenzy that one sees only in certain predatory fish and the media. I can already make out Dr. Melville with his dog at the front of the crowd, but I can't tell whether he's seen me yet. Not that it matters now, I suppose; I've got nowhere to hide.

"Hey, Will. How was your night?"

I look around and see Andrea. She's standing there smiling radiantly, her hair and makeup perfect, the very picture of scholastic excellence. You'd never guess that the last time I saw her she was duct-taped to a chair in the bathtub of a Motel 6, swearing she was going to kill me.

"Hey, look," I say, "about what happened yesterday—"

"No need to apologize," she says, still smiling. Her eyes are positively sparkling, and I see that she's holding a huge cardboard check, like the ones that lottery winners are photographed with after they hit the jackpot. This one reads: TO THE EBEYE CHILDREN'S HEALTH CLINIC, in the amount of $127,770.00. "Just get ready. It's your time to shine."

"Hold it." I look down at the big check, then back up at her. "What are you doing with that check?"

"Giving it to your people, of course. At least, you know,

symbolically." She flicks the hair from her eyes. "The actual money is going into my bank account, where I'll pick it up in cash on my way out of town tonight."

"Wait. You're seriously keeping it?"

"Uh, let's see . . ." she says, putting her finger to her lips in mock consideration. "*Yes.* And, of course, fifty thousand of that money is coming directly from Brandt. Which means—oh, right . . ." She leans forward and whispers in my ear, "This is me beating you."

"Andrea, the bet's off."

"Why, just because you're about to lose? Forget it. You had your chance to bow out gracefully"—she cocks her head and gives me a little smile—"and now you can prepare to wallow in total, humiliating defeat."

"Andrea, wait."

Without another word, she starts winding her way forward with the big check held up over her head. Dr. Melville crosses the lawn to meet her, and when the door of the airport shuttle bus opens, I see a tall, weathered-looking African American man in khakis and a chambray shirt stepping down. It must be Nathan Stanley, the head of the children's clinic on Ebeye. He's clutching the hand of a middle-aged woman who I can only assume is his wife. The couple moves slowly, with the careful determination of people who have traveled a long way and see no point in hurrying now.

I look at Dr. Stanley. There's something about his face that I can't quite identify, something I've seen before, a kind of transcendent peacefulness amid all of this giddy chaos.

I feel a strange tightness take ahold of me as my heart starts to pound. I'm in the wrong place at the wrong time, and it's not getting any easier. A weird silence settles over the moment as Dr. Stanley gestures back into the bus. Two boys, neither of them older than five, come leaping and bounding down the steps, followed by a little girl in a long yellow coat. One of the boys stops in his tracks, eyes wide, and goggles at the fallen orange leaves scattered on the ground. The other exhales, staring in fascination as his breath streams out of him. The girl in the yellow coat squeals and jumps up into the woman's arms. I see Andrea talking to Dr. Stanley and pointing back at me.

"Will!" Andrea shouts, waving me over. "Get up here! Come say hello!"

My heart is pounding so hard that I can hardly breathe. Dr. Stanley and his wife are both looking at me expectantly while their children play around them in the fallen leaves. On the far side of the crowd, I see Gatsby standing there with her arms crossed, watching me through a sea of faces.

Waiting to see what I'll do.

I turn and run.

THIRTY-THREE

WHAT DO YOU WANT?" GEORGE ASKS.

He's just pulled up outside the main security building on the outskirts of campus, exactly where I asked him to meet me when I called him twenty minutes earlier. Now it's almost noon, and the Stanleys have finished their tour of Connaughton's campus and are at the dining hall, where Andrea and Dr. Melville are no doubt treating them to lunch while the TV news crews capture all of the action for the evening broadcast. Meanwhile, George stands in front of his truck, waiting for my answer.

"How would you like to get back at Brandt Rush?" I ask him.

He doesn't say anything at first, just runs his fingers along his long, freshly shaved chin, weighing his answer like a logic problem. "You've got thirty seconds to explain."

"Do you remember a student named Moira McDonald?"

He nods. "Of course I remember Moira. She was a nice girl." He frowns at me. "Why do you care?"

"If you remember her, then you know what Brandt did to her and why she had to leave. I'm giving you the opportunity to settle the score."

"What makes you think I'd help you?"

I reach into my coat pocket and pull out a worn library book, flipping it open to the place I have marked. "In *Foundations of the Metaphysics of Morals*," I tell him, "Immanuel Kant says that when a man tears himself away from his duty to perform any act of altruism, then that constitutes his first true act of genuine moral worth."

"That's a pretty superficial reading of the text," George says.

"Yeah, well, I'm a pretty superficial guy." I look at him. "Are you in or out?"

George doesn't budge. He drops his head, and some of the air seems to leak out of him, deflating his shoulders and chest beneath his uniform. "I can't."

"Why not?"

"Carl."

"What about him?"

George glances back at the truck. "He's the only reason that I took this job."

"I know."

"Did you know that I used to teach on the graduate level?" He rubs his neck and peers back at me as if trying to see whether I understand what he's saying. "You think it's not humiliating, taking orders from Rush? Reporting back to him like some lackey? Knowing that I'm doing this because it amuses him to see me driving around in a security truck? You think I don't hate him for it, every single day?" His eyes narrow. "But this is for my son. I'd love to help you burn Brandt, but . . ." He shakes his head. "I can't take the risk."

"Yeah, you can," Carl says, stepping out from around the corner of the building.

George just looks at him, then back at me. There's a funny look on his face, a combination of surprise and anger. "What . . . ?"

"I asked him to join us here," I say. "Hope you don't mind."

George stares at his son. The boy looks back at him. For what feels like a long, painful time, neither of them moves, and the moment aches like an overworked muscle.

"Carl," George says. But that's all he's got.

"Dad, I don't care about getting kicked out," Carl says. "I hate this stupid school anyway, and Brandt Rush is a total tool." For the first time I see him smile. "Come on. Will and I need to borrow your truck."

By the time we get to Crowley House and George leads us up to Brandt's suite, I've figured out most of the rest of the plan. Not all of it, but the big parts, enough to know what needs to happen next.

George uses his master key to open the suite, and I send Carl in alone. A moment later he comes back and nods at us.

"He's not there. Must still be in the hall shower," Carl says. "We've got time."

Carl and I slip inside, crossing the main room to where the coffeemaker is still brewing up freshly ground French roast.

"You sure this stuff is real?" I ask, glancing down at the vial that Carl brought with him.

"I think so," Carl says. "Dad said he confiscated it from

some kids last month." He hands it over to me, and I can tell something's bothering him. "Hey, Will?"

"Yeah?"

"I'm sorry about hitting you in the face with my lacrosse stick. And punching you. And throwing you against the wall."

"I'm sorry too." I bump fists with him. "We all make mistakes."

Lifting the carafe, I pour half the vial into the coffee. Carl and I duck out of the room, all three of us heading back down the hall to wait in the stairwell. Within five minutes, the bathroom door opens and Brandt comes up the hall with a towel wrapped around his waist and goes into his room. Music starts blaring inside—some kind of hip-hop anthem—and Brandt is singing along through the closed door.

Suddenly the voice stops. The music keeps playing, but Brandt's not singing along with it anymore.

I don't actually hear the thump, but I'm pretty sure I feel it. It sounds like a giant falling to earth.

I look at George and Carl. They look back at me.

"Game on," I say.

We carry Brandt down the stairs and out to the truck in his towel and lay him in the back. He's not quite unconscious —he keeps mumbling and drooling on himself—but he can't seem to move his arms and legs or open his eyes, which makes everything a whole lot easier. George covers him up with a blanket.

"Where to now?"

I hesitate. Up until this point, my thoughts have been running a mile a minute, but they have finally collapsed at the side of the road to catch their breath.

Then Carl smiles. "I know the perfect place."

THIRTY-FOUR

B Y THE TIME I MANAGE TO UPLOAD THE PHOTO ONTO THE
school's website, I'm pretty sure the drugs have worn
off. It wasn't a particularly heavy dose to begin with,
and although I'm not around to see the details, I'm picturing
Brandt waking up on the floor of his suite sometime around
three p.m. with a throbbing headache in his skull and the
sound of someone—maybe several concerned someones—
pounding on the door.

When his parents got my anonymous email linking
them to the Connaughton homepage, they must have pan-
icked and phoned Dr. Melville, because it was the head of
school who called George and demanded to meet him in
Brandt's room immediately. I can speculate about this part
with some confidence because it's George who describes the
scene to me later that afternoon, while he and I are gathered in his truck with Carl out by the statue of Lancelot
Connaughton.

"Did he see the picture?" I ask.

"I don't see how he could've missed it." George grins, looking down at my MacBook, where the official Connaughton
Academy homepage now features a full-screen, high-resolu-
tion image of Brandt, stark-naked, duct-taped to the statue of

Lancelot Connaughton. You can't actually see anything R-rated because of the way we wrapped the tape, but Brandt's got a big, dreamy smile on his face, and the message below the picture couldn't be more obvious.

TO BRANDT,

SO GLAD YOU COULD FIND THAT "SPECIAL SOMEONE" TO MAKE ALL YOUR DREAMS COME TRUE!

MOIRA

"Moira McDonald." Looking at the screen, George chuckles and glances at me. "You know, signing her name to that was a stroke of genius."

"Thanks," I say. "It just seemed like the right thing to do."

"They'll kick you out for it," Carl says.

"No doubt." I nod. "It was worth it. Especially the part where we got to yank the tape off him before he woke up."

"He's probably still counting what's left of his chest hair," Carl says.

George shakes his head and laughs. "Wherever Moira is," he says, "I hope somebody sends her a link to this page before the administration takes it down." He casts a sidelong glance my way. "Hey. You mind if I ask you something?"

"What?"

"You're the new kid on campus. You haven't been here a month. You didn't even know Moira." He frowns and nods at the screen. "So why are you doing this?"

"I need something from Brandt," I say, "and this is the only way I could get it."

"What?"

Before I can say anything, my cell rings. On the other end, Brandt is apoplectic, so furious that I can practically feel the spit flying through the earpiece.

"I got the cash," he shouts. "Two million. Tell your boss we're coming back. I'm going to take that piece of crap down *tonight*." I hang up the phone without responding.

George cocks an eyebrow. "What was that?"

"My long-lost buddy," I say, holding out my hand for George and Carl to shake. "It was a pleasure working with you, gentlemen."

Something tells me I won't be seeing them again.

THIRTY-FIVE

N HOUR LATER, I'M WAITING NEXT TO THE STATUE OF
Lancelot Connaughton when Brandt comes striding
up with an expensive-looking leather briefcase. His
jaw is clamped and his eyes are slits. Any sign of playfulness
is gone from his face now. Even in the twilight, I can see that
he's squeezing the handle hard enough to make his knuckles
go white.

"Where's your driver?" he snarls.

I glance at my phone to check the time. Six o'clock. "He'll
be here." Clearing my throat, I look down at Brandt's briefcase and say in a lower voice: "He's, ah . . . he's not sure Mr.
McDonald can cover a bet that big," I say. "Two million is a lot
of coin. There might be a house maximum."

"Too bad," Brandt says. "Your boss shouldn't be running
an online casino, then, should he?" He pokes me hard in the
chest as if the message requires additional punctuation. "Don't
wuss out on me now, Humbert."

Seconds later, Uncle Roy pulls up in the Caddy. This time
Brandt doesn't wait for me to open the door. He practically
leaps into the back seat with the briefcase on his lap and we
head across campus. Uncle Roy drives in silence. Out the window I see tiny dots of white swirling down through the street

lamps. It's starting to snow. Brandt pops a couple of ibupro-fen. His phone chimes and he ignores it. We keep driving, the lights on the highway flashing by us in the oncoming night.

"Been meaning to tell you," Uncle Roy says from the front seat, glancing in the rearview mirror. "I like that picture of you and your pal online."

Brandt stiffens but doesn't say anything, and I think I can actually hear his back molars grinding together. By now his grip on the briefcase is enough to permanently dent the leather.

"I gotta say, though," Roy continues, "that statue must've been pretty cold, huh?"

"You want to shut your mouth, old man?" Brandt says. "Or maybe I'll come up there and shut it for you."

Roy eyes him. "You try."

"Guys," I say, "take it easy, okay?"

Roy returns his attention to the road. Brandt holds on to his briefcase. When we arrive at the office space in Lowell, he jumps out and heads up the stairs. I follow closely. On the landing, I put my hand on his shoulder.

"Hold on," I say. "When we get into McDonald's office, let me talk to him first. I think he'll let you make the bet, but I just want to be sure."

Brandt ignores me, shrugging off my hand, and barges through the door. Inside, it's business as usual — Rhonda on the phone at the reception desk, smoking a Camel and working on her nails, programmers at their computers in the main office. Brandt walks past all of them and slams his briefcase onto the nearest empty desk.

"Somebody get me a laptop." He looks around, whipping his gaze back in my direction. "Where's your boss?"

Across the room, the private office door opens and Dad comes out. First he stares at Brandt, and then he looks at me, pointing one accusatory finger in my face.

"I thought I told you not to bring that piece of crap around here again."

I take a step back. "He wants to make a bet, Mr. McDonald. I tried to talk to him, but he's got cash in hand—"

"How much?" Dad asks.

Brandt dials in the combination on the briefcase and pops the latches, opening it up to reveal rows of cash, neatly stacked and bundled. "Two million."

Dad stares at it for a second, then shakes his head. "It's too much. I can't cover a bet that big."

"That's what I tried to tell him," I say, "but—"

"There's nothing on your site about a house maximum," Brandt says. "Which means you have to take this bet." He steps forward. "And by the way, you can tell your daughter I said that she can go to hell."

Dad glares at him. Something twitches in his jaw. Then he looks at me.

"Get him a laptop," he says.

It's Lupo Reilly who brings the laptop over and sets it up next to Brandt's briefcase full of cash. Brandt sits down in front of it and Lupo hovers nearby, next to Dad. All the crew members are watching out of the corner of their eye, but Brandt's too distracted to notice. Next to the briefcase, his iPhone sits there, turned on, screen up. Brandt logs on to the poker site, and Lupo takes possession of the briefcase, then clicks in his credit — two million in cash. Dad and I are standing five feet behind Brandt, just far enough back to get a full view of everything as it happens.

The hand gets dealt. Brandt looks at it and places his bet.

"Wait," Dad says. "You're betting the full two million on one hand?"

"Maybe I'm feeling lucky." Brandt glances at the iPhone and then at the laptop, where he trades in two cards.

I look at Dad. He looks at me. I'm aware that I've been holding my breath for a very long time. I can tell Dad's just as nervous.

Brandt looks at the phone again, then back at the computer screen. I try to swallow but my throat's too dry. A single pin-head of sweat prickles against the right side of my rib cage. Brandt's finger hovers over the return button, suspended there in space.

Two million dollars.

One tap and the money's ours.

That's when I hear the door fly open behind us.

"Don't do it, Brandt."

It's a girl's voice, one I would've recognized anywhere. We all look around at once, and I see Andrea burst into the office in a flurry of papers.

"Andrea?" Brandt gapes at her. "What the—"

"This whole thing is a scam." She points at Dad. "That's not Mr. McDonald—it's Will's father. There is no online poker site. They're about to take you for two million dollars."

Brandt's mouth falls open, and for a brief, shining moment, all the wealth and entitlement drain away, leaving a pale, shocked kid caught with his pants around his ankles. For that instant, however short-lived, it's almost more gratifying than the money.

Then he goes for the briefcase.

"Forget it," Dad says, blocking the way, but Brandt manages to grab the handle of the case anyway. Dad rounds on Andrea, lunging for her with both hands. She steps neatly back out of his reach and fires a glance in my direction.

"The police are on their way," she says.

I stare at her. "I can't believe you did this. I stood up for you in front of Melville."

"Noted and appreciated," she says. "It's time to do what you do best, Billy. Run away. New Jersey awaits."

I take a step back, but my legs don't work. They seem to have disappeared underneath me. I can see Andrea and Brandt heading for the door, and that's when Dad makes his move, throwing himself at Brandt and trying to yank the briefcase from his hand.

"You're not leaving with—"

Brandt whirls and slams the briefcase into my dad's head, knocking him backwards. The case flies across the room. On the other side of the office, Rhonda is on her feet, lips drawn down in a rictus of panic. *"Frank, no!"* She reaches into her purse, and the world goes into slow motion as I see the automatic coming out, swinging toward Brandt and Andrea.

Rhonda fires.

Brandt ducks.

Andrea doesn't.

THIRTY-SIX

OR A SECOND NO ONE CAN SPEAK—OR IF SOMEONE DOES, I
can't hear a sound. The gunshot seems to have cracked
reality itself in half. My dad is the first one to find his
voice.

"What . . . ?" He's staring down at Andrea on the floor,
blood splattered across her white blouse, and then he looks up
at Rhonda. I can see the whites all the way around his eyes.
"What did you do?"

"I didn't . . ." Rhonda manages, and the words seem to
trail off into silence. The air around us smells like gunpowder.
With a blankness of expression, Rhonda looks down at the
gun in her hand and forces the next few syllables out. "Frank, I
thought . . . you said . . ."

"You stupid cow. What the hell were you thinking?" Dad's
face has now gone white with alarm, and he stares at me.
Sirens are rising in the distance, getting closer, and I can see
him trying to remember every exit. "This isn't happening."

Meanwhile, all I can see is Andrea.

She's sprawled out below me, pale and motionless, staring up at the ceiling, and I think of the way that Mr. Bodkins
described her to me after my first day at Connaughton. *Looks
like she sleeps in a coffin.* There's a thread of blood trickling from

the corner of her mouth, and her hair is over her eyes. Looking at her, I feel like somebody's kicked me in the chest.

Somewhere off to my right, Brandt is making weird, high-pitched, asthmatic noises, and I can feel him trying to process what's happening, the facts sinking in, and how he can't possibly be here in the middle of this room. I know exactly how he feels. This isn't part of the script. Dad and I were supposed to have Brandt's cash and be out the door by now. Instead there's a seventeen-year-old girl on the floor in front of me with a bullet in her chest, dying.

I think about how this all got started, with a wild, misdirected flight of optimism that I realize now was just a delusion.

It's all gone wrong.

The sirens are right outside now, car doors slamming, and I can hear footsteps, authoritative cop shoes, coming up the stairs.

"Will . . ." Dad looks at me and moves his mouth, but instead of talking, he just turns and bolts for the back office. There's a window in there that is connected to a fire escape, and when he's gone, I notice that Brandt is also backing away.

"I can't . . ." he starts, and turns to go, but it's too late.

Two men in suits are stepping through the doorway. They immediately put Uncle Roy in handcuffs.

And that's how I know it's really over.

"FBI," the tall, bald one says, flashing his badge as he pushes Roy into the corner, while the other agent, a distinguished, middle-aged guy with a well-trimmed goatee, slaps some cuffs onto Rhonda. The bald one rushes over to where Andrea's lying and looks at his partner. "Call an ambulance."

"They're on their way." The second agent turns and scans the room, his gaze settling on Brandt. "Brandt Rush?" he asks, as if to confirm his identity.

Brandt takes a step backwards. The sight of their badges seems to have done something to him, snapped him out of the paralysis of the moment. He blinks at them, hands in the air. "Wait, hold on—"

"Mr. Rush, you need to get out of here right now." The bald agent is moving toward Brandt. "The Bureau has been surveilling this operation for a week, and your father sent us to get you out." He casts another glance down at Andrea. "There's a car waiting downstairs. Come on."

"But—" Brandt looks at the briefcase across the room. "What about my money?"

"There's a dead girl on the floor, Mr. Rush. You can't be mixed up in this right now."

Brandt's eyes widen. "That's two million dollars in there!"

"It's evidence now," the bald agent tells him, grabbing his arm. "Right now you have to go."

As he hustles Brandt out the door, I finally feel whatever was left of my strength draining away, pulling the hinges on my knees, and I manage to descend to the floor so slowly that it doesn't hurt. It feels vaguely reassuring to know that at this moment, I literally can't sink any lower.

The bearded FBI agent walks right past me to where Andrea's lying on the floor. Watching him in action as he squats down to look at her, I realize that there's something familiar about the way he moves. Turning her head to one side, the agent leans down and taps her on the shoulder.

"They're gone."

Andrea opens her eyes and smiles. "You sure?"

"Positive."

The agent helps her to her feet. That's when I remember where I've seen him before. He's Donnie, and the first time I saw him, he was dressed in a bathrobe and standing in my dorm room, claiming to be Dr. Melville while he ordered me to pack my things and leave Connaughton. And the other agent is Chuck, his tall build and bald head helping him pass, apparently, for any kind of authority figure.

Words fail me. I stare at Andrea, and I get a totally unreal feeling that the world is going sideways on its axis. I wonder if this is how a mark feels when he recognizes that he's been suckered, and I realize—however belatedly—how much I've really learned here after all.

Andrea spits out a squib of blood, wipes her mouth, and brushes her hair back out of her eyes, favoring me with a smile.

"Well played, Will," she says. "Sorry we couldn't let you in on it earlier, but we figured it would be more realistic if you didn't know the whole setup."

"*We?*" And now I'm staring across the room at Rhonda, who's already pulled off her dishwater-blond wig and tossed it unceremoniously on the floor. She's actually quite young and pretty if she were to take off her makeup and not dress like a tramp.

The woman walks over and gives Andrea a hug. "We did it," she says, and Andrea smiles.

"Are you going to call Moira?"

"Right now," Rhonda says, and dials a number on her cell phone. "I'll put her on speaker."

The room goes quiet as the phone rings, and a voice— Moira McDonald's, I guess—picks up. "Rhonda?"

"Hi, you," Rhonda says, mock-casually. "Guess what?"

"You got him?"

Rhonda smiles at Andrea. "Nailed the bastard to the wall."

Through the phone, Moira lets out a whoop of pure joy. "I can't believe it," she says. "We finally got Brandt Rush!"

"And then some." As Rhonda takes Moira off speakerphone and continues the conversation privately, I flick my eyes back over to Andrea.

"Who is that?"

"Moira's older sister," Andrea says. "She's a junior at Mount Holyoke."

I stare at her. "So you and my dad actually—"

"Yuck. No." Rhonda makes a face. "Thankfully your dad's a black-out drunk. I just let him get plowed and in the morning I'd tell him what a great time he had."

"How long have you two been planning this?" I ask. "From the beginning?"

"Moira and I were best friends when Brandt put up those pictures of her last year," Andrea says. "I promised her we'd get payback. From the moment I realized that you were a con artist, I knew you'd pick him as a mark."

"I'm seriously that predictable?"

"You're a guy," she says with a shrug. "All you required was the proper motivation."

"So our whole bet was just—"

"Me getting you to do what I wanted and needed." Andrea blinks, the very picture of innocence incarnate. "I guess it worked."

"What about the—"

Bang!

Jerking upright at the noise, I spin around to see Uncle Roy holding a bottle of champagne, bubbles spilling from the neck. It's the good stuff. He's already serving it to the rest of the crew, who have abandoned their computers and are holding up glasses to be filled.

"Were you in on this too?" I ask him.

"Only at the end," Roy says. "Andrea came to me a few days ago with the perfect way to get your dad off your back, and I knew I had to do it." He beams at her. "You're a pretty sharp grifter for a kid," he says. "In ten years you'll be dangerous."

Andrea gives him a crooked smile. "Thanks. I think."

"You too, William." Roy rests his hand on my shoulder, and I see a serious expression come over his face. "Good con. Even if you weren't in on the whole enchilada, your mother would be proud. You're going to be great at this, kid—maybe even better than me someday." Then, before I can reply, he tosses back a glass and turns to the room. "Okay, everybody —have your drink, and start tearing this place down. I don't want to be here when the Rush family comes back with the real police."

"Uncle Roy—" I begin.

"Later, William, all right? I'll meet up with you at the airport with your cut of the take." Turning, he grabs one of the computer monitors and hands it off to Chuck. "Everybody lend a hand—let's get this *done*."

The office bursts into a blur of activity. I look over at Andrea, but she and Rhonda are off in the corner with Moira still on the phone, the three of them laughing and talking about the score. Andrea glances down at the bloodstain on her blouse, and Rhonda points at the gun, reenacting what just happened. In the midst of all of it, Andrea looks up at me and starts walking back over.

"Hey, tough guy." She comes in close, regarding me quizzically. "You all right?"

I nod. "I'll survive."

"Kind of weird to find yourself on the other end of the con, isn't it?" she asks. "But we had fun while it lasted, didn't we?"

"Who knows?" I say. "Maybe I'll bump into you down the road."

She gives me a peck on the cheek and turns away.

And that's okay, because now that I know how it's going to end, I realize that I still have one last thing to take care of.

THIRTY-SEVEN

WILLIAM?" IT'S UNCLE ROY'S VOICE ON THE OTHER end of the cell phone, and he's bellowing loudly enough that I have to hold the device a good six inches from my ear. "Are you even listening to a single word that I'm saying to you?"

"I can hear you just fine." Looking down at the backpack lying open on my bed, I shove the last of my clothes inside, just jeans and T-shirts, and stuff the laptop in before zipping it up. "I'm just not sure why you're freaking out like this."

"You're not sure? You're *not sure?*"

"Well," I say, "I guess . . ."

"The money's gone, kid! Nobody saw where it went! One second we're tearing down the office, clearing out, and the next second . . ." He pauses. *"It's just not there."*

"Yeah, well." I glance out the window of my room, mentally saying goodbye to the view. "I guess you're right. The money's gone."

"You guess?" Roy roars and coughs his incredulity. "William, I'm asking you this once, and it's not a rhetorical question: Who are you, and what did you do with my favorite nephew?"

"Come on, Uncle Roy, face it. It was never about the money."

"Are you nuts? Of course it was!" Roy is coughing louder now, like he just swallowed his cigarette. "And what about those other guys, the ones that came up here from Boston for the job—"

"And they got to work with the most legendary con man in America," I say, "at the very top of his game. They should be paying you."

"Well, yeah," Uncle Roy grumbles reluctantly, "you're right about that. But still . . ." He sighs. "She took off with it, didn't she?"

"Who?" Although I know exactly whom he's talking about. "Andrea?"

"Who else?" Roy growls. "Come on, we both saw the way she and Rhonda were sizing up that briefcase. I don't care what they said about revenge being enough."

"She already took the hundred and twenty-five thousand that she raised for those orphans," I say. "You'd think that would be enough."

"Nuts." Roy grunts. "I don't care who you are—nobody in their right mind walks away from two million bucks."

"I guess you'll be going after her, then?"

"You bet I will. As soon as . . ." There's a long silence, and Roy finally lets out a breath. "Nah."

"Seriously?"

"You know, William, guys like us, we're always looking for the angle, some way to cheat fate," he says. "But in life, as in the big con, sometimes there is no angle. Sometimes you just have to play it as it lays." He pauses and I realize we're reaching the end of our conversation. I stop and take one last look around my room to make sure I didn't miss anything. I've left my Connaughton school uniform neatly folded at the foot of the bed. I don't belong here, and at this point I don't plan on lingering around any longer than I absolutely have to.

I hear the sound of a motor getting louder, and I look outside my window again. A hundred yards away, an airport shuttle bus is pulling up in front of the statue of Lancelot Connaughton.

"Roy," I say, "I need to go. Call me when you get back to Vegas, okay?"

"I'm not going to Vegas, kid. Not right now, anyway."

"Why not?"

"I got a tip on some hot action, a little stock swindle going down in Fort Lauderdale. Florida's where most of us geezers end up anyway, this time of year. After that . . . who knows. Europe, maybe. The French Riviera." He chuckles. "Lots of rich widows there."

I smile, imagining him walking down the café-lined boulevards of Nice, hand in hand with a wealthy socialite from Minneapolis. "Thanks, Uncle Roy. I really appreciate everything you've done for me. This was . . . really great."

"Don't thank me yet, kid," he says. "You hear anything more from the Rush kid?"

"Not really. Word around campus is that his parents pulled him out of school, flew him to Davos for a week on the slopes." I can only shake my head at the absurdity of it. Only in this particular stratum of American wealth would someone get punished for losing two million dollars by being sent on a ski trip. "I think he's probably just glad it wasn't worse."

"Well, do me a favor—see what you can find out about that two million, huh? For an old man's peace of mind?"

"I will."

"It was a good con, wasn't it?"

"The best," I say, and click off the phone, making my way to the door.

Walking down the pathway to the statue, I see Dr. Stanley and his wife walking toward the airport shuttle bus with their three young children, who are all dressed in Connaughton sweatshirts and bouncing happily forward.

"Dr. Stanley?"

He stops and looks at me, his forehead wrinkling in puzzlement as he shields his eyes to see who it is. "Yes?"

"Sir, I know that you don't know me, but I just wanted to say"—I hold out my hand—"that I'm really glad you and your family flew all the way here to visit the school."

He doesn't speak for a moment. "It is very strange," he finally says.

"What's that?"

"My family and I traveled here to your country, and we arrive here with great fanfare, only to find out that all the money that was raised for the orphanage has been embezzled."

"I'm sorry about that, sir." Reaching down, I pick up the briefcase I'd brought and hold it out to him. "I hope this helps."

"What is it?"

"A minor contribution, on behalf of the alumni. In the hopes that you won't remember your visit here at Connaughton as being all bad."

Dr. Stanley takes the briefcase and pops the latches, holding it upright so that the bundles of cash don't go spilling out. "This—" His eyes widen slightly. "How much is this?"

"I believe it's in the neighborhood of two million dollars."

"I—I cannot possibly accept—"

"It's our pleasure." I hold his gaze. "It was good to meet you, sir. I'd like to come visit your island sometime, if I could. In many ways I feel like I already know it."

He just blinks and nods, glancing back at his wife and children, who have already climbed onto the bus. For an instant his eyes hold mine with an unexpected intensity. "Thank you," he says simply. He closes the briefcase and steps onboard the bus, joining his family. The door closes and the bus pulls away, leaving me standing there next to the statue of our founder.

It's time for me to head out too. Shouldering my backpack, I turn around and start walking, making my way to the main gate. It's going to be a long hike to town, but I'm optimistic about catching a ride once I get there.

My pocket buzzes with an incoming text, and I pull out my phone.

It's a photo of a white-sand beach, the ocean blue and rolling in the distance, so clear and bright that the wave peaks look like glass. There's no message, just the picture taken from a beach chair or a hammock, legs with freshly painted red toenails in the foreground. I think I know whose toes they are. And I figure that wherever Andrea's stretched out at the moment, she's a lot warmer than I am, standing here.

I smile. "Good for you," I murmur, and slip the phone back into my pocket.

"Mr. Humbert," a voice says behind me, and right away I know who it is.

THIRTY-EIGHT

I T'S DR. MELVILLE. HE'S GOT HIS DOG, CHAUCER, WITH HIM, and he's growling. Both of them are, actually. "Stay right where you are."

"Dr. Melville . . ."

"You didn't really think you were going to get away with this, did you?" Stepping toward me, he takes out his phone. "No matter. I'm certain that the authorities will be able to clear everything up." He offers me a dry smile that makes tiny creases form in the corners of his mouth. "And I am equally certain that at the very least, you will be going to juvenile detention for a very long time."

"Not if you don't want everybody to know about how the school was sold a fake Gutenberg by your father," I say, but at this point the argument sounds weak even to me, and Dr. Melville literally laughs in my face.

"Please," he says. "Once I'm through exposing you, do you really think anyone's going to care about you and your pathetic accusations?"

He's got a point. And I could outrun Dr. Melville right now, but I can't run forever. I think of my father, plotting and scheming and always looking over his shoulder, hurting the ones he loves. When does it stop?

"I'm not even going to bother taking you back to my office," Dr. Melville says. "We're going to wait right here for the police to arrive. I assume you've got nowhere that you need to be?"

"Not really," I say. "Not anymore."

"I'm glad to hear that." He's already dialing when a voice interrupts us.

"Let him go."

Dr. Melville and I both turn around, and when we do, a half-dozen figures in black ski masks are standing there in broad daylight, with six more stepping out of the trees behind us. Either we've been surrounded by the most clueless group of bank robbers in history, or the Sigils have shown up just in time. Their appearance here is obvious enough that a handful of students on their way to class have already stopped to watch what's happening. Within seconds, the group of onlookers has grown to twenty, then thirty, watching the standoff and whispering among themselves.

Dr. Melville looks like he wants to say something, but his chin just twitches a little while his dog gives a growl.

"What do you want?" he asks.

"William Humbert is one of us," the ski-masked figure in front says, and stares steadily at Dr. Melville. "You of all people should be able to appreciate what that means, Harold."

Dr. Melville flinches a little at the sound of his first name being spoken aloud. "This boy is a criminal and a fraud." He raises his voice so that all the kids standing around can hear him. *"He jeopardized the reputation and integrity of this school!"*

"You did what you had to do to get into this school, Harold," the masked figure says, just loud enough for everyone to hear. "Would you like to tell everyone how *you* got accepted here?"

The crowd stands completely silent and spellbound, waiting. Dr. Melville doesn't say anything, but the expression of alarm on his face tells me everything I need to know. He gets the point. His shoulders sag. He lowers his gaze. The masked figure takes a step forward and holds out his hand.

"We take care of our own," the masked figure says. "Right?"

After what feels like an eternity, Dr. Melville finally reaches out and takes the leader's hand, and the two of them exchange a strange, ritualistic shake. Dr. Melville gives me one last look, then skulks up the path in the direction of his office with his dog padding along beside him. After a few moments, the group of spectators disperses, the students making their way to class.

The ski-masked figure turns to me. "Welcome to the Sigils."

"But . . ." I shake my head. "I gave back the Gutenberg. I failed the assignment."

"There are other ways of proving yourself worthy," he says, then turns and walks away. The others follow suit, silently fading into the trees like a squadron of prep-school ninjas.

All but one.

After I've followed her around the corner of the arts center, where we've got some privacy, Gatsby peels off her mask. Her hair tumbles down over her shoulders. We step back into the light—the midday sun catches her eyes, and she puts on her glasses.

"Hey," she says.

"Hey, yourself." I look around to make sure there aren't any more surprises coming out of the woodwork. "So I guess I should thank you."

"You could," she says. "It really wouldn't be necessary." She glances at her watch, then turns in the direction of the campus. "Walk a girl to work?"

We start down the pathway toward the library, neither of us talking.

"So I have to ask," I begin.

And Gatsby says, "Yes?"

"Melville and his dad . . ."

"What about them?"

"They were con artists too? A father-and-son team? That's the dirt that the Sigils have on him?"

"Well, his father was," she says. "Apparently Melville took the straight path once he arrived here."

"That's . . . encouraging."

"I thought so." Gatsby raises her eyebrows. "Speaking of reforming," she says, "have you heard anything about what happened to Andrea?"

"Well, based on everything I've seen, I can only assume that she took the hundred and twenty-five K and moved on." I take out my phone and show Gatsby the photo that I received a few minutes ago. "This might be a clue. It just arrived on my phone, sender unknown."

"The beach?"

"Looks like the Caribbean. Or Mexico."

"Sounds like her. And you?"

There it is, the question I was not exactly looking forward to. I nod, squinting up at the sky as if maybe there's some wisdom to be found there. "I'm heading out too."

"Where to?"

I shrug. We're standing right in front of the library now. Gatsby turns and puts her back to the door, then looks up at me.

"You don't want to stay?"

"I can't."

"Why not?"

"I don't fit in here. I'm a con artist. I've spent half my life pretending to be someone I'm not."

"Come on, Will." Gatsby gestures around the campus and laughs. "What do you think half of these kids are doing?"

"Yeah, but in my case, it's kind of literally true."

"People change."

"Sure they do." I try to smile, but it feels all wrong and I give up. "I'll see you around, okay?"

"Will?"

I turn around.

"Everybody makes mistakes," she says. "What matters is what you do afterward." Then she smiles. "Thanks for the Hawthorne."

And she turns and goes into the library, leaving me out in the cold.

I stick my hands in my pockets and start to walk away, heading up the path toward the lacrosse field, acutely aware of my surroundings. Students are on their way to class, talking and hurrying along. The bell tower rings, chiming out the hour. Squirrels scamper in the branches.

I walk a little farther, thinking it through. If it's really true that what matters is what you do afterward, then I still have a choice, an opportunity to stop running and start living. Okay, maybe I still can't write a coherent essay on Wilson's Fourteen Points, but I studied harder for that exam than I've done for anything else in my life, and I actually *liked* it. My mind goes back to the guy in the ski mask saying, "Welcome to the Sigils." And I think about Gatsby. If Connaughton really is the second chance I've been looking for, maybe I don't need to con anybody anymore, least of all myself.

Maybe I'll even learn to play lacrosse.

I stop and turn around, looking back in the direction that I came. Before I know it, my feet start moving, carrying me back to the library, and I open the door, stepping into the warmth and the smell of books and the soft lighting.

Gatsby's sitting behind her desk, checking in books. I walk over to her, and she looks up from behind a stack of dusty old hardcovers.

"Listen," I say, "I was thinking, you know, since I'm already a Sigil and everything, maybe it would be for the best if I hung out here for a while." A few students are looking up at me from their carrels, giving me annoyed looks, but Gatsby's just smiling. "Plus I heard there's a secret library hidden within the library, and I was thinking maybe we could find the hidden journals of Lancelot Connaughton. Who knows, maybe the old guy was something of a swindler himself, you know, before he—"

"Will?" Gatsby says.

"Yeah?"

She points to the sign that says QUIET, PLEASE and puts her finger to her lips. And when she stands up and comes around the desk to kiss me, it's exactly as warm and soft as I'd always hoped it would be, and I realize that I'd be perfectly fine standing here with her for the rest of our natural lives, surrounded by the smell of old books. I think about what Roy told me on the phone.

In life, as in the big con, sometimes there is no angle.

Sometimes you just have to play it as it lays.